Autocracy in Democracy

By

Blessing Amu

Auctus Publishers

www.AuctusPublishers.com

Published by Auctus Publishers
606 Merion Avenue, First Floor
Havertown, PA 19083
Printed in the United States of America

ISBN (Print) : 979-8-9894812-3-1
ISBN (Electronic) : 979-8-9894812-4-8
Library of Congress Control Number : 2023950485

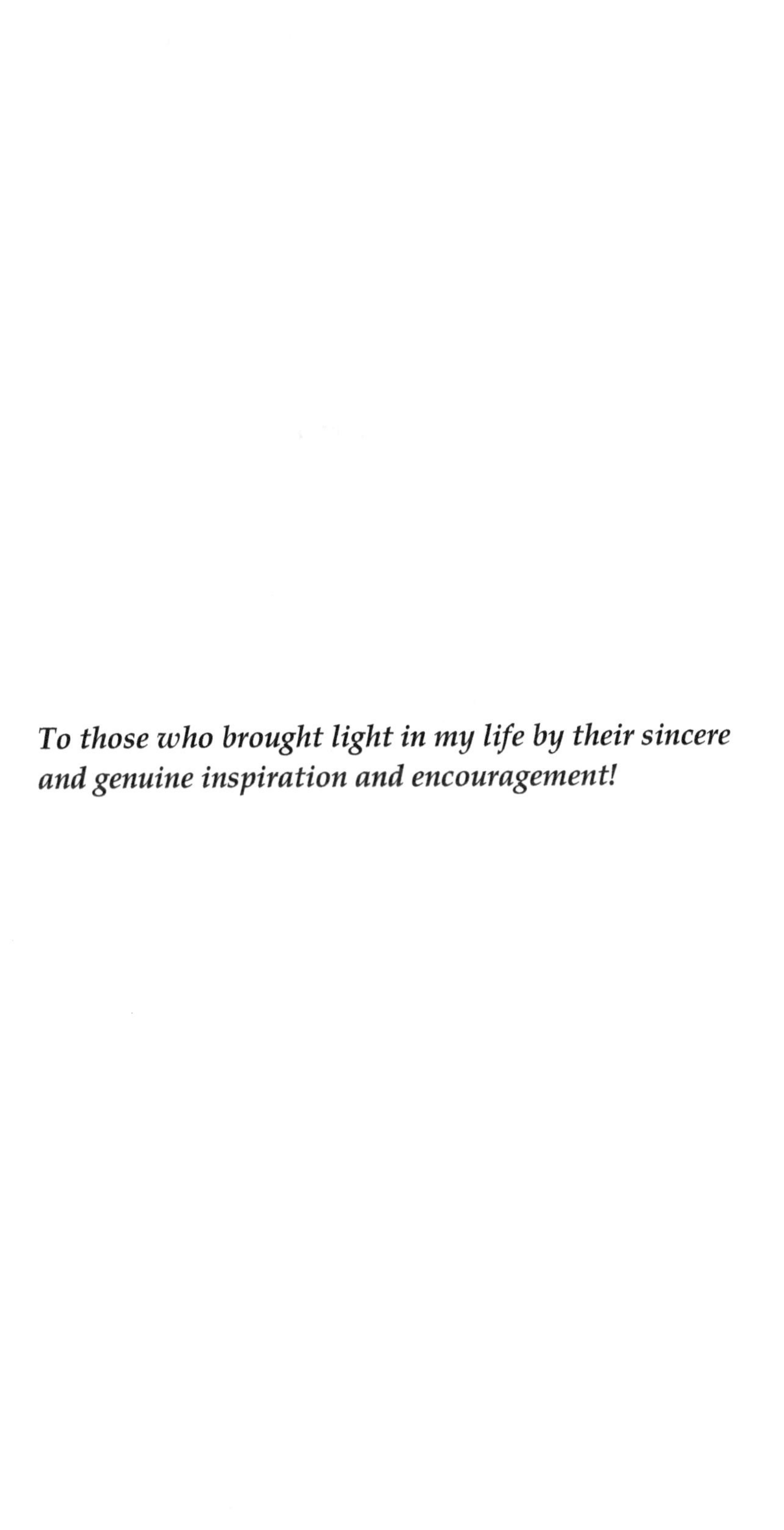

To those who brought light in my life by their sincere and genuine inspiration and encouragement!

Contents

President Anane was so aggressive. His two hands firmly choked Lawyer James' neck. He became impatient as James refused to tell him the whereabout of the documents. He finally released his hands on James neck, and reached for a gun from one of the two bodyguards who were with him. The other bodyguard swept the foot of James and he went to the ground. It was very late in the night, around 1 am, in one of President Anane's warehouse in the outskirt of the city.

"Will you tell me where the documents are, so I spare your life, or you will still be mute, so I put a bullet through your brain." President Anane said.

"The people voted for you to serve them. They voted for you to use the country's resources to serve them better, to create a soft life for the vulnerable. We did not vote for you to come loot our properties." Lawyer James boldly said.

"Listen, James. Don't be stupid! These documents are not worth your precious life. Just hand them over to me and save yourself and your family."

"I don't care what you will do, Mr. President. I am a proud son of this soil and I won't sit idle for you and your greedy officials to create, loot and share this country's fortunes."

A black land cruiser Prado came to park next to them. Two men dressed in black stepped down from the car. One of them went straight to the booth and brought out Mrs. Nkrumah whose hands were tied with rope and her mouth plastered. The guard removed the plaster on her lips and pushed her to join her husband on the ground.

"Where is his son?" Mr. President asked.

"We didn't find him there." The guard replied.

"Find him and bring him to me."

The two guards left again in the black land cruiser Prado.

"Your husband has refused to tell me where the documents are, so I brought you here to tell me… now where are the documents?" Mr. President addressed Mrs. Nkrumah.

"I - I have, have no idea Mr. President." She stammered as she cried.

"Really? I see…then I don't think you are useful in anyway."

"Pooh!" "Pooh!" Two bullets each in their heads. Lawyer James Nkrumah and his wife never begged for their lives. They were people of honor.

Lawyer James was a private legal practitioner who had his own law firm, Nkrumah J. and Associates. He was a human right lawyer who people respected so much because of his honesty and humility. He won many cases. The last case he won before his death was the one between honorable Stephen, an energy minister and one of the President's confidants versus Mister Obed Aggrey, a peasant farmer in the eastern region of the country. Honorable Stephen had illegally sold Mister Obed's fifteen acres of land as a concession to a Chinese company for them to mine golds illegally. Lawyer James took the matter to court and won the case for mister Obed in a probono. In the course of the case, he was threatened severally by the government to distance himself from the case, but he stood his grounds and sought for justice.

Mrs. Nkrumah was a fashion designer who designed dresses for high profiles. She had only a son with Mr.

Nkrumah. Greg Nkrumah was only seventeen years when his parents were killed. His father made him flee to a typical village in the woods the night before their murder.

"Dispose off the bodies." Mr. President said to the guards.

*****

The streets were covered with red. The youths were demonstrating against bad leadership that had brought hardship and suffering to the country. They were not happy at all. It was evident that the New Democratic Party (NDP) that the people believed so much that they could put the country in the right direction by fixing the economy had betrayed them. Indeed, political talk is different from real talk and facts. When the party was elected into office, their problems had doubled. The country took two steps backwards in the wrong direction instead of moving forward in the right direction. The government seemed not to care or did not have the right men for the job. The people hit the street to express their anger through a peaceful "eye red" demonstration. They wore read to symbolized how angry they were.

"Hi, what's your name?" A journalist asked.

"My name is Yakubu." He said.

"Why are you here, why are you demonstrating?"

"I'm demonstrating because of the hardship we are facing in this country. At first, a ball of kenkey was Ghc1.50, but in this current administration, a ball of the same size of kenkey two years ago is now Ghc5. I used to buy toothpaste for Ghc2 but now the same toothpaste is sold for Ghc12… Our roads are very bad, lights go off almost every day, no portable water for people in the rural areas. You see, it seems there is no leader in this country. We cannot sit down and watch these greedy people destroy our country. So, this is why I am demonstrating today."

"Thank you very much Yakubu, for speaking to us. This is Pocu TV, we are streaming live on all our twelve affiliate stations across the nation."

Many others joined the demonstration. The likes of some spare parts dealers, some drivers, some head potters, some market women and etc.

"Hello madam, what's your name, and why are you also demonstrating today?" The Journalist asked one lady.

"My name is Alice. A political science student. We are tired of bad leadership. My mother sells in the market, and my uncle is a commercial driver. My father died when I was still young, so it has been my mother and my uncle who have catered for me and my two siblings till now. Prices of food stuffs have skyrocketed; she cannot afford to buy them in bulk and sell them at the market. My uncle had to pack his car because of the insane increase in fuel prices. It's better the President resigns and steps down."

Another young man intercepted.

"I want to ask where the huge amount of monies they borrow in our names go to? They go for these loans in the name of roads, but our roads are still bad. They take these loans in the name of better hospitals and schools, but we can't see these hospitals and schools. So, we want to ask, where is the money?"

"These are some of the questions the people are asking. Keep watching Pocu TV, I am Astonish, your reporter."

In the presidential villa, the president and two ministers of states were watching the demonstration on the television, sipping glass of wine.

"I think these are the sympathizers of the opposition parties who want to make our government unpopular." The finance minister said.

"This is normal, Nimako. It is their constitutional right. They are just keeping fit on the street; they will go home and sleep when they are tired. Just enjoy their foolishness." The President said.

They laughed. Akosua Anane came to say goodbye to her father, Mr. President. She was leaving for school. She was in level three hundred at the Harvard University in America.

"Learn well, my baby girl. You are going to take over from me when I retire. Safe journey." The president said.

"Take care, my daughter-in-law to be." Finance minister said and smiled.

Akosua smiled too.

"Thank you, uncle." She said.

"Let my daughter complete her course first, after that you can worry her with your son. But for now, she needs to focus." He said and smiled.

"My daughter. God be with you. Safe journey." The information minister said.

*****

It was late in the evening in Mister Bojo's mansion. There was a meeting between few high profiles, some from the ruling party, and some from the largest opposition party. Mister Anane, the President, Alhaji Yussif, the Vice President, Honorable Nimako, the Finance Minister, Honorable Lawyer Albert, the Attorney General, and Honorable Dr. Mavis, the Foreign Affairs Minster. Those from the opposition party were Mister Newman, the opposition leader, Mrs. Vivian Gaisie, the running mate to the opposition party and two members from the opposition party. They often had meetings almost every six months.

Mister Bojo was a man in his early eighties. He was young and strong for his age. Only few people knew him because he was not the man who was out there. A very simple man, he never went out with bodyguards apart from his driver. He was the secret founder of the two main political parties in the country, the New Democratic Party (NDP) and the Freedom Fighters Congress (FFC), a very smart and dangerous man. Both parties were behind the scenes one family with the same father; but they appear as enemies in the public eyes. Nobody knew that secret except those who were present at the meeting. It was like a secret cult. Mister Bojo rules the country indirectly, through these two political parties.

The general elections were near. It was barely six months to the elections. They planned on how to approach the elections.

"You have done a great job with your appointees." Mister Bojo addressed Mister Anane, the president.

"You see, it is always best to make the masses suffer in hardship in the first two years of government, and then in the third year, you make things easy a little. They will start forgetting the hardship they went through in the last two years and begin to have hope that things would be better in the following years. Let them buy into your manifesto. Tell them what they want to hear. Share monies to them on the election day so you can earn their trust. Then finally, rig the election if you can." Mister Bojo said.

Mister Newman looked at Mister Bojo and smiled and said.

"We will be very vigilant and won't allow them to rig the elections."

They all laughed.

"Yes, you should not allow them to rig the election. This will make the act become real. Let the public believe you are enemies. You have to match the governing party boot for boot as an opposition party. Speak for the people, let them have trust in you. Don't forget to throw light on the corruption practices of the government. Let the people know how corruptible the government is - throw light on the petty petty corruptible practices, and not the grave ones." Mister Bojo Addressed Mister Newman.

The electoral commission had been weaponized to endanger the prospects of elections. Because of that, electoral misunderstandings and electoral violence had turned a lot of places in the country into a killing field. There were six registered political parties in the country. Anytime they went for meeting, the electoral commissioner, Dr. Florence Seidu, imposed what she thought was best for her and didn't accept the views of the other political parties. She assumed a certain war-like aggressive penchant as if she had a war with certain individuals of the other political parties.

Dr. Florence was a forty-five-year-old beautiful woman of color. A slim woman with a beautiful shape. She was not all that tall. She had that charming eyes that entice many, especially men.

Dr. Florence had always demonstrated largely that she was a woman of a fragile ego. She did not factor the concerns and the welfare of the people in whatever decision that she made. She felt so emboldened to do whatever she wanted, and never saw the commission as a sensitive state institution which was charged with the mandate to supervise elections to be free and fair and to deliver on the people.

When people with weak ego take positions, they become so much entrenched because they always think when they give up on their decisions and take the opinions of others, they would be seen as weak. That was how Dr. Florence was. She was part of Mister Bojo's secret cult. She was always in bed with the governing party because they were from the same nest. These are vultures who pounced on the country to make their wealth.

On the same day at the studios of Pocu TV, Astonish had an interview with Mr. Jackson, one of the conveners of the "eye red" demonstration.

"People are saying the largest opposition party was the one behind your demonstration, and all that you are trying to do is to paint the government black and make it unpopular." Astonish addressed Jackson.

"You see, what have gone on in this country for us to reach where we are today, every well thinking citizen is concerned. I am aware there are many who would think some of us may hate the government or anything else but where we have gotten now, people should know that we have gone past personal politics and partisan politics. Our demonstration was due to the excesses of unreasonable things we didn't expect them to happen in a civilized democratic dispensation where we have a president who is a self-acclaimed human right lawyer, who is supervising corruption and injustices under his watch. A president who promised the citizens that he was coming to protect the public purse - a president who promised a lean government, but he came and decided to do the contrary. Officially, this country is declared bankrupt that we cannot even service our debt. My brother, this is the true state of the country now. So, our criticisms stem from these facts which are incontrovertible."

"I know you presented your petition to the President yesterday through his secretary. What is next?"

"We are waiting for the President's response in action. If nothing is done, we shall express our discomfort in another better way."

"When you say another better way, what do you mean?"

"I mean another better way… but let me say this, I am appealing to the religious leaders to speak. I am appealing to the chiefs to speak. These politicians come to you to use your pulpits to campaign to your congregation. They come to your palaces and towns to convince electorates. You should not sit idle for this country to be destroyed with the excuse that you pastors and chiefs do not involve ourselves in active politics. The country belongs to us all, and posterity wouldn't forgive us if we remain silent... A German theologian, Martin Niemoller, said this and I quote..."

"First, they came for the communist, and I did not speak out because I was not a communist.

Then they came for the Socialists, and I did not speak out because I was not a Socialist.

Then they came for the Trade Unionists, and I did not speak out because I was not a Trade Unionist.

Then they came for the Jews, and I did not speak out because I was not a Jew.

Then they came for me, and there was no one left to speak out for me."

"I see. So, you mean this country's crisis is not only because of bad people but the silence of good people as well?" Astonish asked.

"Exactly my brother. And Osagyefo Dr. Kwame Nkrumah, the first President of Ghana once said something. He said. *"If change is denied, or too long delayed, violence will break out here and there. It is not that man planned or willed it, but it is their accumulated grievances that shall break out with volcanic fury."*

"Thanks for coming, Mr. Jackson."

"Thanks for having me."

Chapter 2

Some years passed. Greg Nkrumah, the son of lawyer James Nkrumah lived in a typical village which was situated in the middle of a forest in one of the typical villages in the rural area. He had taken a wife, Mrs. Akyere Nkrumah, who was a native of the village. The village was not populated. There were only about sixteen families living little far away from each family on a vast land. Their main occupation was farming and hunting. Opanin Bobi was the father of Mrs. Akyere Nkrumah. He had thirteen children with his four wives. The first wife gave him six children, he had two children with the second wife, one child with the third wife, and then four children with the fourth wife. Nine males and four females in all. Opanin Bobi was eighty-six, eating into his nineties, still strong. He lived with his two wives on the same land but far from where Akyere and her husband settled. His two wives, the first wife and the third wife, had died. Akyere was the only daughter of his third wife. Three of his thirteen children had died separately some years ago, two males and a female.

The village was named after Opanin Bobi. So, it was called *"Bobi-kuma." "Kuma"* means *"Junior."* He was named after his father's brother, Okyeame Bobi. So Opanin Bobi became a junior "Bobi" to Okyeame Bobi, hence earning the name "Bobikuma," to wit, "Junior Bobi."

Greg Nkrumah was in his late thirties. His wife Akyere was in her thirties too. They had an only son named Kwabena Nkrumah, who was five years old.

Greg and his wife sat on a wooden bench under a mango tree in their compound. There stood a wooden radio box next to Greg. They listened to the news, while little Nkrumah played on the ground.

"There has been a coup d'etat just an hour ago. President Newman have been overthrown by the military over his incompetent to govern the nation. The coup took place just this morning in the presidential villa. President Newman has been detained in the presidential villa. Two of his security guards were killed in the operation. Today, people are celebrating what looks like the end of Mr. Bojo's dynasty, the faceless father of the two biggest political parties in the country. Mr. Bojo was shot at his residence when he tried to flee after the coup..."

"Mr. Bojo?" Greg asked.

"Do you know him?" Akyere asked.

"Yes I do. He was a simple man, yet very rich. He was the best friend of President Anane."

"The man who killed your father?"

"Yes."

The radio was still speaking…

"The movement which brings together all the companions of the defence and security forces has decided to put an end to the regime you know, on the 12th of March 2001. The decision taking will enable our country to get back on track. The boarders of the country are closed until further notice. All the institutions of the republic are dissolved, the government, the parliament and the constitution of course. We call on the population for calm and serenity. Long live our homeland!" Said, the leader of the coup.

"That was Major General Yussif Mohammed, the leader of the coup." The reporter said in the radio.

Greg was so quiet. He sat in a deep thought. Akyere looked at him and decided to break the silence.

"This country is rich in many natural resources. We have gold, diamond, bauxite, lithium, oil, and the list go on and on yet we are the poorest in the world, what at all is wrong with our leaders?" Akyere said.

Greg looked at Akyere, smiled and said.

"Poverty is a multi-billion industry deliberately created by these cruel politicians to enslave the population."

"So you mean these politicians intentionally make us poor?" Akyere asked.

"Listen, one politician said to my father, which I still remember because I was right there when he said it. He said, if you want to enslave the population, take away their economic freedom and they would be forever indebted to you. This is the reason politicians share things like, cup of rice, bar soup, maggie cubes, secondhand clothes and some cheap stuffs to the masses for vote buying when there is an election."

"God will punish these useless and selfish politicians. I am happy the military has taken over now."

When night fell in each day, around 12am, there was another city in the city which erupted with their own rules, with their own system and how they behaved. Young men wielded guns at the ghettos, young ladies involved in prostitution and drugs just to end a living. All these happened in the heart of the capital of the city. These young talents lived such lives of desperation but in the estates, politicians enjoyed better lives with their families. They didn't care about the voter.

The journalists who were supposed to speak for these youths, they allowed themselves for the politicians to buy their conscience with money and cars. The few journalists who decided to speak truth to power were threatened and attacked. For over some years, all what the people saw was a mediocre government. Roads were bad but they still collected road tolls. Water bodies were destroyed by illegal mining activities known as "galamsey", politicians misappropriate funds meant for projects and they were allowed to get off scot-free.

It was about six months since the military took power. Because of the sanctions the African Union and the international community placed on the country, things became very difficult compared to the previous situation. The youths couldn't hold their patience and therefore hit the streets to demonstrate. They never cared about the military. Major General Yussif met the youths himself and warned his soldiers not to touch anyone of them. He stood on his land rover car so the youth could hear him well.

"Thank you all for your boldness. Indeed, I was waiting for you guys to stand up for the development of this country without fear or favour, and you have just done that. I am very happy. I am sixty-two years, and I will be leaving soon but this country belongs to you. Yes, I and my colleagues were not happy with the way the previous government was running the affairs of this country, I spoke, and I overthrew the government. I never saw the true picture- I am now a president and I am seeing the true picture of the problem, though the African Union and the international communities have decided to make things difficult for our country. I know you are very concern about development... please, everybody should go to his or her home, and let's have a renewal of mindset that we have only this country, and this country is what we have. I Major General Yussif Mohammed, there are things I may not have taken into consideration. So I am pleading with you now, that whatever you want me to fix, please list them and bring it to me so I can go through. Moreover, let each of us here, irrespective of any decent job we have, should work in truth and honesty because we have only this country. I stand here today and promise you that I shall hand over power to a civilian government in three months' time."

The youths fell in love with the Major and applauded him. The leader of the demonstration thanked him, and they dispersed.

Akosua had planned with Nimako to form a new party. The National democratic Party and the Freedom Fighters congress had been dissolved by the military. The military had promised to hand over power to a civil government in three months' time. Mrs. Akosua Nimako took it upon herself to form a new political party that could win power and form a new government.

She was a hard-core type but her husband was a calm person.

"Are you sure this is going to work?" Mr. Nimako asked.

"Why not? Why are you doubting?"

"Are people not going to say, our parents were part of the problem and that there won't be anything new we would bring on board?"

"And who said I am going to contest for the presidential position? I said I am forming a political party."

"What is your plan?"

*****

Akosua, the daughter of the former President Anane, and Gideon Nimako, the son of the former Finance Minister had already tied the knot. They were blessed with a daughter. President Anane and his wife died two years ago in a motor accident, when they were returning home from a meeting. They had gone for a meeting in Mr. Bojo's mansion about an oil deal contract they wanted to sign with an Australian company. He was a former President then, but he was the one who introduced the deal to Mr. Bojo and to the current President. President Anane was looking for a five-percentage kick back, but the unfortunate happened.

People said the oil discovery was a misblessing to the country. Because they had sold all their gold fields to foreign companies and they were not benefiting anything, and still their lands were being degraded. They were afraid the oil would take the same trend. These leaders thought about themselves alone and not the country. How could a whole one hundred and twenty-five parliamentarians approve three percent share on what they got from lithium while the foreign company that mined it took ninety-seven percentage?

*****

In the village of Agona Bobikuma, the sight of the green plantation gave one a heeling view. The atmosphere in the woods were so therapeutic. The chirping of the various birds were so nice and melodious to the ears. It was very difficult for someone to fall sick in the village due to the natural therapeutic environment. They ate fresh fruits, vegetables and foods straight from the plants. They did not have any pipe borne water to drink from. They dug the ground and made a pond for themselves. These ponds were usually created under big trees, so they were not directly exposed to the sun. Anytime the atmosphere became hot, the pond became cool to calm the burning body system. They did not consume any artificial chemicals as most of the people in the city often consume.

It was Ama Mansa's marriage ceremony. A younger sister to Akyere. Mansa was the second child of his father's fourth wife. The family of Ama Mansa's husband had already came for the knocking, and it was time for the marriage itself. Every custom had it own procedures in marriage. Agona Bobikuma being an Akan land, when a man was interested in a woman and had the intention to marry her, he would first have to propose to the woman for acceptance. After that he would go to see the woman's family with his family and laid his intentions before them. They would not go empty handed, they would go with a bottle of schnapps, distilled alcohol and a pot of palm wine.

The father of the woman would call the woman and tell her the man's intentions and asked her whether he should accept their gifts of items. If the woman said yes, her father would then accept the gifts and would give them a date to come for the marriage list.

The woman was said to be engaged after her family had accepted the man's gifts. The man would go for the marriage list at the specific date and would also give the woman's family the date he would come and perform the marriage rituals and to pay for the woman's bride price.

Amuzu and his family were at the compound of Opanin Bobi to pay Mansa's bride price and performed the necessary marriage rituals. Every single soul of both families was there to witness the occasion.

After the ritual, Amuzu and Mansa were declared husband and wife by Mansa's uncle. Alcoholic drinks and soft drinks were served to grace the occasion.

It was Friday evening in the city. Fridays were for pleasure. That was where bars, restaurants, and any entertainment places became crowded. There were sounds of different genres of music along the streets. A black Toyota venza entered the gate of Nimako's house. Nimako's house was situated just hundred meters away from the street.

Reverend Enoch Stephenson stepped out of the car. Mr. Nimako met him and led him to his hall where the meeting was taking place. Mrs. Akosua Nimako had already formed her political party. The Victory Peoples' Congress (VPC). The meeting was about how they were going to win power in the following month in the general election. Dr. Festus oware was the presidential candidate who the

Victory Peoples' Congress had presented as their flag bearer. He was a very intelligent, smart and highly respected personality who had his PHD in economics.

Reverend Enoch was one of the financiers, and who helped the party to garner more votes since he had a church of about thousand congregation.

In the heart of the city, in one of the biggest hotels conference hall, people were seated listening to the presidential debate. The debate was between the four presidential aspirants of the four political parties. The Victory Peoples' Congress (VPC), the New Dawn party (NDP), the Freedom congress (FC), and the Patriotic Development Party (PDP).

"Gentlemen, can you explain to us in a minute, what your vision for the country is in terms of the economy. Beginning from the presidential candidate of the VPC. Dr. Festus Oware." The moderator said.

"My vision of this country is a shining example of what we as Africans can achieve when we manage our affairs well. Our institutions must work again, and therefore VPC offers a return to the path of building a self-rindge economy that gives the best living conditions for its citizens. In the pursuit of that development agenda which we will enshrine in the constitution to ensure continuity from one administration to the next which has been a vital missing link in our development. We will be able to deliver free maternal care...."

"Your time is up please. Mr. Bismark Nkrumah form the NDP, you are to answer the same question please. You also have one minute."

"We the NDP believe in good governance. We believe in leadership of transparency, tolerance and togetherness. The NDP will deliver free quality education and retrain our human manpower by investing in the national economy. We will ensure that our natural resources are exploited for the benefits of our country and our people. We will directly and indirectly invest in agriculture to drive the economy and also ensure that our own entrepreneurs are giving a competitive advantage in our marketplace."

"It's now the turn of the Freedom Congress through their presidential candidate, Dr. Llyod Kwesi Nkrumah to express their vision for the country." The moderator said.

"The vision of the Freedom Congress is the vision I fully subscribe to, and it is the vision of this country as a thriving democracy. A country where the rule of law and the respect for human rights are entrenched in the way which we do business. Not only a democratic state but also a prosperous state…"

He started coughing. The moderator asked him to take in water. He took the water, yet coughed more. They went on recess.

In the following month, the general elections were held and the New Dawn Party (NDP) emerged winner and ruled for two consecutive terms.

Chapter 3

It was almost 11 pm in the night. A muscled man, dressed and posed as a guard, stood by the door of a parked SUV on the almost empty road. All the shops on the stretch were closed and there was little to no activity that went on. The SUV was parked with just a few other cars visible in the distance ahead.

It didn't take long when Beatrice modeled on. She wore an all-black three-piece dress that showcased her elegance and form. Beatrice was in her mid-twenties and very gorgeous. She looked way too young for someone of her age and when we say sauce, that was right there.

She was not happy, and the pace at which she approached the car made that clear. As soon as she got to the car, the muscled man opened the door for her. Another man stepped out of the car's driver's seat and left Beatrice in the back seat of the car with Mrs. Akosua Nimako.

Mrs. Akosua Nimako was a forever young woman who refused to grow into her early seventies. She had style, and she was very eloquent and confident, and the tribal mark under her right eye made her stand out even more.

"It was you, wasn't it?" Beatrice asked in an upset manner.

Mrs. Akosua Nimako looked at her with a wild eye.

"Kill that base in your tone before I do it for you," she warned.

Mrs. Akosua Nimako had this natural authority in her voice that automatically conjured respect from whoever she was talking to.

"I told you I have everything under control," Beatrice said in a soft voice.

"That was what you said but didn't look like that to me. I was running out of time." Mrs. Akosua Nimako explained.

Beatrice got worried. She was the only one who knew what was going through her mind. She broke her silence.

"You should have told me something. What am I supposed to do now?" Beatrice complained.

Mrs. Akosua Nimako, who was busily pressing her phone, sharply replied;

"Nothing! It's my show from now onwards."

Beatrice looked at her and asked.

"Just like that? All my work is in vain."

She was very upset, but she needed to control it because she was not talking to anybody other than Mrs. Nimako.

"No, darling. All your work is the reason we are where we are..." Mrs. Nimako replied.

"It makes little sense. Why..." Beatrice intercepted. But Mrs. Nimako had already decided, and nothing Beatrice would say would make any difference.

"I'm doing what is best for us all," Mrs. Nimako hinted.

Beatrice looked at her for so long that their eyes instinctively locked.

"No. You're doing what's best for you. That's what you always do." Beatrice told Mrs. Nimako.

She stepped out of the car and banged on the door. Mrs. Nimako entered a moment of thought.

*****

A flashback of a vast stretch of green vegetation. Fresh crops are strategically planted in different regions of the farm. The atmosphere was serene and the sound of the tree branches as they danced to the melody of the wind made it even more calming. Nkrumah, an athletic, handsome boy of age ten, had his already loaded catapult. He walked in a stealthy mood, trying his best to make little to no sound. He had no slippers on. In the near distance was an enormous tree, flooded with different birds chirping. He found a suitable spot, aimed his weapon at the tree, and then fired.

The birds scattered as the catapult fired. He listened carefully and heard a sound. Bingo! A warm smile formed on his face. He got one.

A few moments later. Nkrumah walked on one side of the lane on a dusty road, with trees and vegetation on both flanks. Various farms were visible. He walked with his catapult around his neck like a necklace. In one hand was the bird he got from his hunting, in another was an orange he was eating. He walked a little and then came toward him a car, traveling at quite a speed. He looked at the car in admiration until it passed him. The clouds of dust that were following the car from all that speed made it a little difficult to see who was in that nice, fancy car. But he waved at it, anyway. He continued his journey, enjoying his company.

Nkrumah got to his parent's farm. In their small wisdom, they had made something that looked like a tap where they washed their hands and got some water. Nkrumah washed his hands. "Papa," he called out to his father. Surveying the area, he instinctively moved towards where he suspected they could be... He got there, only to find his mother and father lying on the ground, soaked in blood. He came to an immediate halt. The bird dropped from his hands, tears ran down his cheeks as he looked at them, dead.

A grown Nkrumah, in his late thirties, sat in a prison cell looking at nothing, reminiscing. He was almost teary. In his cell with him was an old man in his early eighties. At that moment, he was singing an old Akan song. A sorrowful one. His husky yet rusty voice and the pain in the way he sang the lyrics reflected all that he was feeling and gave a goose-bumpy atmosphere to the cell room.

Nkrumah soaked in the song, sunk deep into his thoughts, reflecting on very painful times. He tried his best to fight the tears, but they overpowered him. A blink, and tears came rushing down his face.

The sun fell onto the faces of the inmates. Nkrumah was still awake. It looked like he had no sleep. Nimo was fast asleep, snoring peacefully.

"You! Up. Someone is here to see you." An officer told Nkrumah.

He opened the gate and waited for Nkrumah to came through. Nkrumah was a little confused and took his time.

"Get moving, boy. We have things to do." The officer said to Nkrumah.

Nkrumah came to the door and was put in handcuffs. He then followed the officer.

The officer brought Nkrumah into a special room. A well-suited man, Eric. Who was around the same age as Nkrumah, stood there waiting for him. The officer brought him to his seat and left him there.

"Hi. Nkrumah." Eric greeted.

Nkrumah did not retaliate against the rather welcoming smile Eric had on.

"Who are you? What do you want?" Nkrumah asked.

"One at a time. Who am I?... My name is Eric Mawuli. We have never met, so don't worry about your brain trying to recall where you know me from… What do I want.?"

Eric looked at Nkrumah for so long that he caught his eyes and made the perfect eyeball-to-eyeball connection.

"I want to help you," Eric said.

"The only help I need now is to get out of this hell."

"I don't know if I mentioned it earlier, but I am a lawyer and that's exactly what I am here to do," Eric said, and then took his seat.

"My hands are tied and there is very little I can do for you, Nkrumah."

Nkrumah looked into his eyes and then looked to his left to see nothing there.

"I don't know what you have been told. But I swear to God I didn't do it." Nkrumah confessed.

"Whether you are guilty is not what is in question. Are you familiar with the proverb that says the disobedient fowl obeys in a pot of soup?" Eric asked, but Nkrumah did not respond.

"What about the one that says, where water is the boss the land must obey?" He added.

Nkrumah was still looking at him, not sure what was going on. But Eric kept on speaking in proverbs. He finally came clear to Nkrumah.

"Okay, what I'm trying to say is that your case, this one," Eric said and pointed to the table.

"Let's just say it's a game, okay? And we have already set the rules. You need to play according to the rules or it's game over. The people who brought you here want to make sure you remain here for as long as they want and, as illegal as that sounds, they can, and they will." Eric addressed.

"So you believe I'm not guilty?" Nkrumah asked.

"I am a lawyer. Not a judge." Eric replied.

Nkrumah was silent, still looking at Eric. He was confused a little about what was going on. He didn't want to say much.

"Nkrumah, right about now, only you can help you. Where is it hidden? That's all they want to know," Eric said.

"I have said it a thousand times. I don't know…"

Nkrumah didn't finish what he was saying, and Eric intercepted him. He hit his right hand hard on the table and was more aggressive.

"God damn it! They will kill you, Nkrumah. They will hurt you. And they will do it slowly that your soul will beg to leave your body. They will tear apart every single vein in your body and they will ply out all your fingers."

Eric stood up and walked slowly around Nkrumah as he continued talking.

"They will wear you a crown of thorns and press it down your skull till your face is soaked in your blood. They will kill you. And it will be so painful you won't even have time to cry. The sad part is, there's no stopping them. Because they own the ones who own the ones who can help you. That's how insanely cruel your case is. It's the way or no way."

Eric said and sat back in his chair. Nkrumah said nothing. He looked straight at Eric with a straight face. Eric breathed out heavily and then breathed in. He calmed himself down.

"Okay, okay. You look like a man who has made your mind up. As your lawyer, it is my responsibility to inform you that you are to be transferred to a private holding facility." Eric said.

Nkrumah smiled confidently and threw a question.

"Are you a Christian?"

Eric was born into Anglican. His parents were all Anglicans. But it was a decade since Eric went to church.

"I am not a regular churchgoer, if that is what you are asking. But yes, I am a Christian." Eric replied.

"Then you should know that the Lord fights for his children," Nkrumah said.

Eric looked at him and smiled.

"We will see about that. Please reconsider your decision. Both our lives depend on it. Tell them what they want to hear," Eric concluded.

He picked up his bag, and then hurried to the door where he banged. The officer shortly came to open the door and Eric left.

"Alright boy. Time to go. Up!" the officer told Nkrumah and took him back to his cell

C h a p t e r 4

It was daybreak. A very muscled guard guided Nkrumah, who was in an all-blue kit, a little oversized. They walked in the middle of two cell lanes. About five on both sides. The place was serene and quiet, and, unlike the typical prisons, the occupants of the cells looked nothing like rascals. He walked until he got to the very last cell on the right. The guard opened the door, and he entered.

"Welcome to hell, boy." The guard teased.

He locked the cell door and left, whistling.

"Don't let the quiet fool you," Kwame said to Nkrumah.

Nkrumah turned around to see his roommate, Kwame. Very intelligent man entering his seventies. He was fit and healthy and looked nothing his age. His gray hair was the only thing that gave him away.

Kwame came to his feet and paced towards Nkrumah and offered a hand.

"Kwame." He introduced himself.

Nkrumah hesitated a little, but put his hand in for the handshake, eventually. And also mentioned his name to Kwame.

"Once again, welcome to hell," Kwame said to Nkrumah.

Nkrumah and Kwame were in the middle of a conversation.

"...I don't know how to make this clear enough, but the only way you are getting out of this hell is in a body bag," Kwame told Nkrumah.

Nkrumah looked keenly at Kwame, who was lecturing. One talkative he was. He continued...

"The worst is that you don't get even a befitting burial."

"None of that is fair. How is that even legal? I had no trial. They can't just dump me in jail. Especially for something I didn't do." Nkrumah said.

Kwame giggled. "Baby boy. There's a lot of learning to be done. Do you think anybody here did anything? No. We were all dumped here because the government wants us here. With our mouths shut and our influence erased. Every single person here at a point tried to expose or speak against the government."

"What about your families, your friends, your lives?" Nkrumah asked.

"All of that ended as soon as you walked in here. There is no going back, boy. To the outside world, you are dead. And that is the only way you get to walk out of this place, dead."

Nkrumah asked, "So, why are you here?"

"Same reason you are here. I found out too much. I threatened to expose Mrs. Akosua Nimako and her corrupt VPC. They have murdered and tortured and done everything possible to keep that seat. And they have no intentions of giving it up." Kwame asserted their plans.

"No. That's not why I am here. I am here because one psycho I have never met thinks I have information I know nothing about."

Kwame stayed quiet for a moment. He spoke after a brief moment of reflection.

"So it's you..." Kwame calmly asked.

"Me? What do you mean it's me?" Nkrumah was puzzled.

A guard came to hit their cell door.

"One more word from this room and you are both going to scrub. Get to bed." The guard warned.

They said goodnight to themselves. Kwame fell onto his wooden pallet, designed into bed. No mattress, just the woods. He left Nkrumah even more confused than he was before.

Some days on. Nkrumah and Kwame were seated on their respective beds. A tray comfortably sat on both their laps. On each tray was a bowl of porridge and bread. The food looked nothing attractive, but they had no other choice but whatever they brought to them. Kwame, who had gotten used to prison food, found it more comfortable. Nkrumah, on the other hand, was disgusted. He was playing with the food when he should be eating.

Once in a while, he raised his head and tried to make eye contact with Kwame, but Kwame didn't even look in his direction. He was head down and concentrated on the food. Nkrumah broke the rather awkward silence after he had had just about enough.

"You know you haven't said a single word to me in three days."

Kwame finally looked at him a bit, then he was back concentrating on his almost-done food.

"What did you mean by it is me?" Nkrumah asked.

Kwame sighed audibly. "Tell me your story, boy."

"My name is Kwabena Nkrumah. I am from Agona Bobikuma. At age ten, I was forced out of my hometown into the city."

"What happened to you?" Kwame pushed further.

"I went to my father's farm to meet him dead. Both my parents. I was supposed to be there with them, but I quarreled with my mother, so I didn't go. Instead, I went hunting. I got a bird. I intended to hand it to my mother in exchange for her forgiveness."

He paused, then he continued.

"I heard a gunshot from nowhere. I panicked. I started running as fast as my legs could carry me. I run and run and run. The only place I knew was my hometown, and I had to run from it. No idea where I was going, but even at that age, I remember it like it happened yesterday."

Nkrumah was all emotional. Kwame was listening carefully, with eyes filled with sympathy. He continued...

"I woke up the next morning with a broken leg in a hospital. I was told a car had hit me. That is how I ended up here. I lived with this ex-serviceman. The man who knocked me down. He heard my story and offered me shelter."

A warm smile covered Nkrumah's pain as he reminded himself of his dead guardian.

"He loved it when I called him General. I lived with the General for twelve years until death came knocking. His children and grandchildren wanted me out of the house."

He sighed...

"You can't blame them, but I was old enough, and I had made a little money, so I moved out."

"May his soul rest in everlasting peace," Kwame said.

"Good man he was. I got myself into the university. Schooling part-time, working part-time. Graduated with a second class lower. Then I met her. The love of my life. She gave a purpose to my life. She gave me a reason to keep moving. She showed me how it felt to be in love. The best thing that ever happened to me. I moved in with her. We've been together for five years. We started getting these weird emails, telling us how they would make our lives miserable. They kept asking me to disclose where it was hidden. They hacked my phone and my personal computer. Everything. It was a torture. I reported to the police, but nothing. But I think they succeeded, because here I am in prison for a crime, I knew nothing about. I don't know what the government wants from me."

Kwame looked at him and shook his head.

"The only conclusion I can come to is that the government was behind all those threats. Which makes you pretty special. Look around, everybody is here because they want our mouths shut. You're here because they want you to open your mouth," Kwame said.

Kwame's statement surprised Nkrumah. He gave a 'what do you mean' facial expression.

"About what? I don't know what is going on. I do not know what they are talking about. How am I to give them information I don't know? For God's sake, I don't even know them." Nkrumah said.

Kwame leaned back, clearly thinking about something. Then...

"You remember when I said the only way people get out of here is in body bags? I have a feeling about you. If what I am thinking ends up being what is, my goodness, you will be the beginning of a revolution."

Nkrumah looked at the smiling Kwame. As if to ask "Huh, what the hell is going on?"

At the spa, Abigail, an elder sister to Beatrice, was lying on the stretch being messaged by a few girls all in bikinis. The spa had a very erotic setting. A soothing country song played in the background as Abigail enjoyed her session. A few moments in, Eric entered. He was feeling a little uncomfortable and out of place. He looked around at all the skin at his disposal. One girl went to whisper into Abigail's ear.

"Leave us," Abigail commanded.

The heavily endowed pretty girls modeled out of the room, making naughty faces at Eric. One of them went as far as running her hand down his chest.

"You have news for me?" Abigail asked, and Eric nodded.

"Good or bad?" Abigail followed up.

"Neutral," Eric replied with little hesitation.

Abigail giggled and then sat up. She was charming and had a very appealing personality.

"My dear, there is no middle ground to this. There is the good, and there is the bad. Everything else is just us trying to convince our minds not to pick a side... But of course, you didn't come here for a philosophy lecture. So, start talking." Abigail addressed.

"I did what you asked me to," Eric said.

"Aww… sweet. And?"

"He didn't fold," Eric replied.

This forced Abigail onto her feet.

"What do you mean he didn't fold?"

"He didn't give out any information. He is still insisting he knows nothing about it." Eric said.

"And you believe him?" Abigail asked with a doubtful face.

After a while of thinking, Eric replied…

"Honestly, I do. He sounds clueless, missing. He does not know what I was saying when I said it"

"Maybe he is playing games with you," Abigail suggested.

"Abigail, I am a lawyer. A bloody good one. I have won you case that no one else could. I never get played. I play the games."

Abigail was not buying any of that. She paced in frustration.

"No, no, no. You promised you would get him to talk." She reminded Eric.

"I know. I am working on it. This kind of thing needs trust. Give me some time." Eric assured.

"Time? Eric time! Time is the last thing we have, and you know it. If anybody else gets to it before us, we are screwed." Abigail cautioned.

"If he knows it. Trust me, I will find it. But I don't think he does. If possible don't move him." Eric advised as he tried to convince Abigail.

"That is not a decision I can make."

"But why?"

"Why? Because my mother thinks I am worthless. She feels I am only book worthy. She doesn't think I am fit for this kind of thing. My opinions are thrashing towards her. That is why. And that is why I am so desperate to get this done. So that I will have something to my name. I am sick and tired of playing junior sister when I should be in charge." Abigail cried out.

"I understand how important this is to you."

"Good. You should also remember you are indebted to us."

"I will get this done. Trust me," Eric assured.

*****

In the Newsroom, a news anchor was seated in a beautiful news set. Makeup was doing a final touch on her face.

"Okay, clear my set for me." The news director commanded. Everyone got into position.

"We are on in 5, 4, 3, 2 and action!" The news director said.

"Good day, ladies and gentlemen. Welcome to the midday news on Shelsea TV. My name is Akosua Safowaa. News reaching us is that the Victory People's Congress, VPC, is holding a closed-door meeting among the party's advisory body to elect the presidential candidate to lead them to victory in this year's election. My colleague, Kweku Asante, is standing by at the party's headquarters. Kweku over to you." The news anchor highlighted.

Kweku Asante was standing on the premises of the party office, where other reporters were present and reporting in the background. He was a very charismatic and athletic young man.

"Thank you, Akosua. Behind me is the headquarters of the Victory People's Congress. The party has been in government for a record of four terms. Per the Constitution, a president can only rule for two terms and that has made this important that the VPC choose a strong candidate to lead them into their campaign as they look to stay in government for four more years."

He paused. He looked to be listening to something in his ears...

"Okay," Kweku said and signaled the cameraman to follow him to the gate of the premises where the other reporters had all rushed to. He continued with the details.

"We hear that the lioness herself, the founder of the VPC, Mrs. Akosua Nimako, has arrived at the premises."

A lot of police, military, and private security personnel who shielded her in the building surrounded Mrs. Akosua Nimako, dressed in the party colors.

"That was Mrs. Akosua Nimako. The fearless leader of the VPC. She has been faced with a lot of scandals and accusations over the years and anybody who loves their news knows that she is in the middle of a lot of rumors in the country. All the other members of the advisory body are already inside, and the meeting should begin soon. As and when we get updates from inside, we will inform our cherished viewers." Kweku Asante detailed.

*****

At the car park of Shelsea TV. Mrs. Morrison. A woman entering her fifties. Very pretty and rocked her fifties look well. She was heading to her car when Kweku Asante came running after her. He caught up just in time to deny Mrs. Morrison the opportunity to get away.

"Kweku, we already talked about this. It's still a no." Mrs. Morrison was straightforward.

Kweku had in his hands some white sheets with handwriting on them.

"Madam, I edited it. Lowered the tone. Trust me when I say this is what we need." Kweku tried to convince Mrs. Morrison.

"I have been here long enough to know that if you want to keep your Media House running, you keep the VPC out of the news." Mrs. Morrison had learned.

"All I need is your permission to publish this story. I will put myself in the firing line for anything that comes after this," Kweku Asante said.

"You are a promising young journalist, Kweku. But if you want to have a job for a long time, you need to be careful with the stories you choose. It's still a no."

"I am fully aware of the risk I am taking. But that is what journalists do, right?" Kweku challenged.

Mrs. Morrison took a long look at Kweku, wondering how a person could be so stubborn.

"Kwame lots, Astonish, Gideon. Find out what happened to all these names. Then, you come to talk to me... Why can't you waste your time on other things like a regular young adult? Journalism doesn't have to be risky. Have fun. Go to the beach, watch some adult movies, Netflix, and chill. Enjoy your life, Kweku. You should not always give your head to the sword."

"Can you at least get me a representative for my show?" Kweku pleaded.

"Oh God." Mrs. Morrison whispered.

"I will see what I can do. And make sure nobody sees whatever nonsense you have in your hands. Burn it. Or use it to wipe your ass. Anything at all, but don't dare show it to another soul." She sat in her car and drove off.

Kweku watched the car until it was completely out of sight. Then he hit the pages on his head several times, frustrated.

"Damn it, damn it, damn it. Damn it."

It was morning at Mrs. Nimako's house. The glamorous house had an even better dining hall setting to complete it. The amount of luxury on display showed just how wealthy and powerful this family was.

Mrs. Nimako sat at the table together with Abigail. A few uniformed house helps patrol in the back getting a thing or two done. Bodyguards were also positioned at spots that were visible from the dining hall. They barely said a word to each other. It was more than obvious these were two people who weren't on the same wavelength.

Beatrice rushed in shortly...

"Sorry, I am late." Beatrice apologized.

She made herself comfortable. One maid came to the table and tried to serve her.

"It's fine. I have got this." Beatrice said. The maid nodded gently and left. Abigail cleared her throat.

"Mom, I want to discuss..." Abigail said, but she didn't complete her sentence before Mrs. Nimako overlapped.

"Abigail, no business at the table." Mrs. Nimako cautioned.

"I know, it's just..." Abigail tried to explain but Mrs. Nimako shot her the "Are you still talking" look and at once she was intimidated. Her mood dropped.

"I am sorry," Abigail apologized.

"Just finish your food." Mrs. Nimako said. The place went back to quiet.

Moments later, after the dining, they were all seated in Mrs. Nimako's office from home. The office was designed with party and national colors and a coat of arms hung behind her. She sat behind a desk. Opposite her were Abigail and Beatrice.

"All I am saying is, you can't give someone dog treatment and expect him to be open," Beatrice said.

"Are we even talking about the same thing here? That guy is a time bomb. And we are the very people seated on top of that bomb. When he goes off, so do we all." Abigail said.

"What do you suggest then?" Mrs. Nimako asked.

"Eric has the situation under control." Abigail notified.

"Abigail, Eric will be needed for the campaign. We can't have him on something like this," Mrs. Nimako clarified.

"He is our best chance at getting him to speak," Abigail said.

"Our best chance is bringing him home and following him. We are working too hard on this case when all we should be doing is working smart. We've been on this for five-plus years. Come on, guys. We are losing." Beatrice opened up.

"Beatrice is right." Mrs. Nimako said.

Abigail rolled her eyes and looked away. It was not like she was expecting to win a debate with Beatrice, anyway. Especially when their mother was the judge.

"He is still insisting he knows nothing. But I know that's a lie…"

"Abigail, how is it going with the finance minister? Is he doing like we asked? Mrs. Nimako inquired.

"It still needs work, Mom. But I will finish the paperwork soon." Abigail assured.

"My girls… I am expecting both of you to be at your best game this year. If there is any year we can lose this seat, it's this one. I am counting on you two angels to make sure that doesn't happen. No matter what it takes." Mrs. Nimako said.

Abigail and Beatrice stood up to leave. Beatrice was first out of the room and right after, Abigail closed the door behind her and she stormed back in, matched straight to her mother's desk.

"Do you like me?" Abigail furiously asked her mother.

"Excuse me?" Mrs. Nimako was puzzled.

"Beatrice, is your favorite daughter, right?"

"Young lady, it's your mother you are talking to!" Mrs. Nimako responded.

"You don't like me. You never have." Abigail cried out.

"Where is this coming from...?" Mrs. Nimako asked.

"Since childhood, you've always favored Beatrice over me. You always give her the main stage while I sing back up in the background, cleaning after her mess. I am the older one. It is me you're supposed to be grooming to sit in that chair, not her." Abigail cried.

"Okay, that is it. That's enough nonsense for one day. What do you want? What is all this about?" Mrs. Nimako said.

"I need you to give me a chance to prove myself. I want you to see me as you. I want to prove myself. I want to show you that I have the stomach for this kind of thing. I want to matter." Abigail pleaded.

Mrs. Nimako wore an evil smile. Nodded slowly at Abigail.

*****

At the private prison facility. Nkrumah sat on his bed. He watched Kwame who had his face hidden in the book he was reading. The silence was broken after a while.

"Is it interesting?" Nkrumah asked.

Kwame lowered the book to show his face.

"The book you are reading, is it interesting?" Nkrumah asked again but this time a little louder.

"Depends. Who is asking?" Kwame responded and asked.

Nkrumah just looked on, unsure of which response to give.

"It's happening to you," Kwame said.

"What is happening to me?" Nkrumah was puzzled.

"You are losing your mind. That's the first sign of surrender. You lose your mind and then question every single thing you have known all your life. Then, someway, you think you are to be blamed for all that is happening and then you convince yourself, maybe I deserve to be here... Don't let that happen to you, boy. Don't lose your mind," Kwame said.

The cell door opened almost immediately after Kwame completed his words. The guard heard that last line.

"You. Up. Follow me." The guard said and pointed to Kwame.

Both prisoners looked at each other, confused. What could happen? It was a very odd time for a guard to come for anybody.

"May I ask why?" Kwame asked the guard.

"No, you may not. Come on up. Don't let me force you, sir." The guard replied."

Kwame came to his feet and even though scared, he followed the guard out. The guard didn't lock the door after they exited which made things even more creepy for Nkrumah.

"Hey, excuse me..." Nkrumah said as he moved toward the door. Right when he got to the entrance of the ajar door, two muscled masked men met him and pushed him back in.

"I - think - you have the wrong cell..." Nkrumah said, panicking.

Baam! A punch into the pretty face of Nkrumah. The punch was so heavy that it took him to the ground almost immediately. The second man closed the door and joined the other. They kicked and punched and brutally beat up Nkrumah who did nothing but cry as he slowly got weaker.

Nkrumah struggled. Blood dripped down his mouth and nose. One could barely recognize the man on the floor. The men did not stop. One went as far as sitting on the helpless Nkrumah and punching the hell out of the little life left in him. They afterward left him lying on the ground. He could barely open his eyes. Face swollen, cuts all over. The masked men walked out of the room and locked the cell.

*****

It was evening on the premises of Shelsea TV station. Eric was in an interview with Kweku Asante. They went on a commercial break.

"Okay, in positions. We are on in 3, 2, 1, and action." The news director commanded.

"Welcome back from that short commercial break. I am still here with lawyer Eric Mawuli, a member of the VPC's communication team. You're still watching the citizens watch. Join us live on Facebook or send your questions to our Twitter handle @citiwatchgh..." Kweku introduced and turned to Eric.

"Lawyer, before the break, you told us some accomplishments of your party and why you think you are the right ones to carry the country forward. Some people think the economy is stagnating and for us to move forward, we need a change in government, fresh ideas, and personnel. What do you say about that?" Kweku asked.

"Well, you know what they say. You don't change the winning team. People are entitled to their opinions, but one thing they should understand is that there is a reason why we've been re-elected in power for four consecutive times." Eric replied.

"Interesting that you have mentioned that. There have been reports and rumors of election rigging and malpractice. The VPC itself has been labeled internationally as a corrupt government..."

There was a fast food corner alongside the street. People were in the queue buying food. A LED TV was mounted on the wall where people were watching the interview.

"I am happy that you mentioned rumors. I once heard I have three nipples. Does that make it true? My brother, people will talk. People will try their very best to paint the darkest of images possible, and that's politics. At the end of the day, when you look at our track record and accomplishments over the years, you will realize why we are one of the most efficient governments on the continent. Not to brag, but Mrs. Akosua Nimako has put together a very strong team of leaders and winners, and that is why we keep winning. Because one who is destined for power doesn't have to fight for it." Eric explained.

"Well said. Now to a rather disturbing matter. Seven months to the election. Two months to the close of submission and we still don't have an opposition, Lawyer Eric?"

"The answer is simple. They are scared. I mean, this is a party that has proven themselves. Nobody wants to waste money on a campaign that has no future."

"What exactly are they scared of? The fact that they will lose, or the fact that every single strong opposition flag bearer over the years had either ended up missing or dead? What people call the election year curse." Kweku boldly asked.

"The election year curse is nothing but a theory. People die every single day. It's unfortunate that members of the opposition or the other die. But that is just life. If they had died any other time but the election year, would it still be called a curse?" Eric asked.

"There are theories that also point all these at you, your party. And there is a trend that keeps repeating." Kweku said.

He seemed to end with his statement.

"I'm listening?" Eric said.

Kweku continued...

"Everybody who have dared to talk about the VPC for what they are disappeared mysteriously." Kweku completed his statement as he revealed.

"And what exactly are they?" Eric asked.

"Cheats, criminals, and murderers." Kweku boldly responded.

The audacity of Kweku Asante gutted Eric. Every crew member in the room was in a state of shock.

"Is this interview live?" Eric asked, wondering.

"It's live and colored, Lawyer. Do you have anything to say against any of these accusations?"

"Like I said. Rumors are rumors. A seasoned journalist like you should get your facts right before you say things you can't prove." Eric replied.

"Oh, I can prove them. Every single one of them." Kweku challenged.

"Okay, that's it. I cut the footage." The director said and marched angrily to Kweku's desk.

"What the hell are you thinking?" The director furiously said.

"I am doing my job," Kweku replied.

"Your job is to ask the bloody questions we've asked you to ask."

Eric smiled confidently.

"You've bitten more than you can chew, boy. See you around. Eric threatened.

He picked up his belongings and walked off.

"God damn it Kweku! what have you done?" The director yells at him and then turns to the crew.

"Show is over. Play music videos. Let me take care of this mess."

*****

Night fell at the private prison facility. Kwame was at the gate of their cell, banging into it. In his hands was a soaked towel. Seated on the floor was a small bucket.

"Hey! I need new towels." Kwame said, but there was no response.

"Can anyone hear me...!" Kwame yelled again.

"We are trying to sleep." A male voice responded.

"Go to hell, Kirk!" Kwame yelled.

The gate opened almost immediately. The guard threw a towel straight into the face of Kwame. He was not happy.

"Anything else?" The guard asked.

"Warm water, some medicine, and food," Kwame replied.

"Your job is to patch him up. You don't get to choose what he needs. Let me not hear you disturbing again." The guard cautioned.

"Else what?" Kwame challenged.

"Disturb one more time and you will find out." The guard challenged.

He closed the gate and walked out. Kwame then turned back to Nkrumah, who was lying in bed in a lot of pain.

"At least I tried," Kwame said to himself

He went to kneel by Nkrumah and continued to clean up his cuts.

"Kwame..." Nkrumah called.

"Whatever you want to say, save that energy," Kwame advised Nkrumah.

"Tell me your story," Nkrumah said.

"My story? What good will that be to you? I will tell you a better story. One I should have told you earlier," said Kwame.

He then came off his knee and sat on the edge of Nkrumah's bed. He started...

"I went to Agona Bobikuma, your hometown one time to cover a story of illegal mining activities, what we call the "galamsey." To everybody else, it was just a story. But I knew some part of me just knew that I would find something that would end the VPC. Because I had had enough. Everybody has actually. There is just nobody confident enough to speak up. The few of us that dared, here we are... Locked up far away. Perceived dead by everyone in the outside world."

Nkrumah coughed, and the pain he went through just to cough was, seen all over his face. Kwame continued from where he stopped.

"Easy boy, easy... At Agona Bobikuma, I met a man. His name was Paul. Paul told me the exact story you told me. The day your parents died; Paul was there. He told me what he saw, and he wanted my help to find you. That is why when you told me your story, I just tore up. I am a strong believer that life works for its highest good. And I believe everything happens for a reason. Right about now I am more than convinced that all my years I have been here waiting for this moment. All I went through was for this exact moment. You and I are in the same cell room talking about what happened to your father. There was something your father wanted you to know, but Paul wouldn't say. I don't know how or when you will get out of here, but if you do find him, he has all your answers." Kwame revealed.

There was a moment of silence. Kwame finally broke the silence and continued.

"Your grandfather was a lawyer, boy. I know this because he was my father's friend. I went to Agona Bobikuma to find him. Your grandfather gave your father a chest filled with documents. Documents that show that all the VPC's properties were illegally obtained. There were two parties formed by one Mr. Bojo. The VPC inherited those illegal properties from. If those documents are leaked, it will cripple every one of them and it will prove every single allegation raised against them. That is what I went to find in Agona Bobikuma. That is why I am here. That is why you are here, too. They are cleaning up, and they're doing a hell of a good job."

The gate opened again. The guard brought the bucket of water and some bananas. He left them at the entrance.

"Go to bed. All of you." The guard commanded

Chapter 6

It was almost midday at the premises of the Shelsea TV station. A convoy of three cars drove onto the almost empty car park of the premises. Police and Military personnel came out of both the front doors and the back doors and got into strategic positions.

Mrs. Nimako stepped out of the second car, flanked by two other personal guards. She stormed straight into the building. Bypassed everyone without saying a word till she entered the editor-in-chief's office.

Mrs. Morrison raised her head and there was this surprise on her face. She came to her feet with such great haste. Mrs. Nimako signaled her to sit. Mrs., Morrison who was already intimidated and shaking went gently into her seat. Mrs. Nimako made herself comfortable too.

"Wel - com…" Mrs. Morrison said with a shaky voice

Mrs. Nimako raised her hand to instruct Mrs. Morrison to be quiet.

"Leave us." Mrs. Nimako said as the two guards who came in with her left her alone with Mrs. Morrison.

"I know you know why I am here. You have five words to defend yourself." Mrs. Nimako was straightforward.

"Trust me, ma'am. I had no…" she didn't end her sentence and Mrs. Nimako overlapped.

"I said five."

There was a long pause.

"You embarrassed me, my spokesperson, and the entire government on your show." Mrs. Nimako said with anger.

"With all due respect ma'am. The presenter only asked questions." Mrs. Morrison defended.

"And made accusations. One that citizens didn't take lightly. Have you seen what is happening on social media? Mrs. Morrison, for Christ's sake, this is an election year and you know how wild things can get. You've been here long enough to know that it is very bad timing to bring things like that up."

"I am sorry ma'am." Mrs. Morrison pleaded.

"I waited for three days for an apology from your Media House and there was nothing. You are aware mistakes like this can't go unpunished... Where is he? The presenter, that one. Where is he?"

"He hasn't been to work since the other night's incident. No one has heard from him." Mrs. Morrison replied.

"Change that. Find him and deliver him to me very healthy and smiling. The last thing I need right now is under missing journalist who is in the spotlight. In the meantime, your media house has been closed down. You seize to operate the very second, I walk out of this place. We will reinstate you in due time." Mrs. Nimako said authoritatively.

"You can't do that. The free press law wouldn't allow that." Mrs. Morrison fought back.

"We will see about that." Mrs. Nimako said and smiled.

She stood up, heading out...

"I will take you up in court." Mrs. Morrison challenged.

Mrs. Nimako who was almost at the door, turned and wore an evil face.

"I am the law. I am the court," she teased Mrs. Morrison.

The frown face of Mrs. Nimako became a smile almost immediately.

"Have a good day Miss Editor. I will advise you to find another job." Mrs. Nimako teased.

One of the guards opened the door for Mrs. Nimako and she gracefully exited. Mrs. Morrison quickly dialed a number.

"Where are you? Get the hell out of town now!" She said on the phone and cut the line.

She was upset and furious. She scattered the papers that were lying on her desk as she screamed. She topped it up by kicking into the desk and hurting herself.

*****

The weather was a little cold as the sun emitted its gentle rays early in the morning. Abigail walked out of the State of the Arts gym facility holding a water bottle in one hand, and a phone in another. A small bag hung across her shoulder. She was dressed appropriately for a morning gym session and her choice of bright colors was on display yet again. She had her face buried in her phone as she smiled to herself when...

"Miss Abigail," Selas called

Abigail raised her head to see Selas. It looked like he was at the gym too. Selas was a well-built man, mid-thirties maybe, tall, charismatic, and exuded nothing but admirable confidence.

"Who is asking?" Abigail said.

"Selas." Selas replied.

"Hi Selas, how may I help you?" Abigail asked playing nice.

Selas pulled out a phone. Did a thing or two.

"Nothing. I think you look familiar. Is this you by any chance?" Selas said.

Then he showed a video to Abigail. Abigail looked completely surprised and scared all at once.

"How did you get this?" Abigail questioned.

"I am getting to that… I work with an eye in the sky. If you love your expose you should know who we are. I will be straight up with you. We are working on a case to bring down the whole VPC. Your family included. We are this close to finalizing this. It's going to be big. Let me give you an exclusive. It's titled twenty years of feeding off fear. Cool right? What do you think?" Selas said and smiled.

"What do you want from me?" Abigail asked puzzled.

"Yeah! There we go. You're speaking my language now. I need you to be my inside person. And I am pretty sure you already know how this will end when you say no. Your mother thinks you are shit right? Wait till she sees these videos… That's right. I said videos. There are more where this came from. Keep your phone close baby. I will call you. You better answer when I do."

"Are you blackmailing me?"

"I am working. You call it blackmail; I call it work."

Selas winked and seductively licked his lips. And then turned around, left Abigail rooted to the spot. About five steps in and he came back.

"Sorry, I forgot. Do you know our motto? I mean eye in the sky. Well guess what, I don't know too. Because we don't have one." Selas teased.

He began to laugh; thought he cracked a good joke. Abigail's facial expression made him realize how much he was overdoing the whole thing. The laughter slowly vanished from his face.

"Sounded funny in my head trust me. I wish you were in my head. But you are not, and I am not in yours." Selas said.

He made his hand a gun, aimed at Abigail and... Pheeew... He made his exit.

The same evening, Abigail walked down a very quiet lane. She walked carefully, looking around every single chance she got. You could see the fear by the way she walked and conducted herself. She made a right turn beside a corner shop. Selas leaned against the shop.

"Going somewhere..." Selas asked.

Abigail who didn't notice Selas as all her attentions were focused on the road in front, got startled. She immediately stopped at her pace, with her eyes closed. In her mind, her end had come.

Selas then burst into laughter...

"Oh my God." He laughs out

"Jesus Christ." Abigail cried out. She was visibly panicking. She placed her hand over her beating heart.

"I should have taken a picture." Selas teased.

"You scared me, what the hell? That almost killed me." Abigail complained.

"I am sorry. I didn't mean to." Selas begged.

Abigail still hadn't gotten herself together. Still in a state of shock and panic. It gave her an at-once headache.

"'' What the hell. Jeez." Abigail yelled.

"Calm down. Deep breathe. Do you want a hug or something?" Selas tried to be romantic

"Just... a second. Please." Abigail said.

Selas thought maybe, he overdid it. Abigail didn't have the stomach for that.

"Yeah. Sure. Take all the time you need. We can go sit in my car if you want... you know what, come on.

Selas held Abigail's hand and took her into his car which was parked a few walks away from where they were standing. Selas handed a bottle of water to her. She gulped down the bottle of water till it was empty.

"Feeling better?" Selas asked.

"I think so. Please don't ever…"

Selas overlapped.

"Lesson learned. First and last time." Selas promised.

"Thirty thousand." Abigail bargained.

Selas was lost.

"Sorry?" Selas asked.

"For the videos. Thirty thousand if you hand them to me." Abigail said.

"It's not really about the money, Abigail," Selas replied

"Fifty. Mention your price." Abigail continued to bargain.

"Price?" Selas asked again.

"Look, I have already given you enough information. What more do you want from me?"

"Cooperation. Get it at the back of your head that I have no interest in making your wild sexual escapades go viral. It will make great headlines; I am not going to lie but the only headline I care about is the one I am going to make when my team and I finish this story. The last piece of this puzzle is you, Abigail." Selas threatened.

Abigail went quiet, thinking.

"If we are going to do this, I will need assurances." She proposed.

"Let me hear them," Selas said.

"I need my family's name out of your story," Abigail said.

"Your family is the story," Selas replied.

"The VPC is the story. When you make the expose about the party and minimize the blow on my family, I will give you something even better. Ever heard of the underworld?"

"The secret society that allegedly runs and calls the shots over the continent?" Selas replied.

Abigail nodded affirmatively.

"My oh my. Just when I thought today couldn't get any better." Selas said.

*****

The night was still young somewhere along the street. Beatrice was seated in her car singing along to a jam playing on her stereo. She was enjoying herself and had the time of her life. Her performance was quickly interrupted by Eric, who jumped into the car and banged the door. Eric was not a happy man.

Beatrice turned off the sound immediately. Also, not happy

"Bro. You could have knocked." Beatrice told Eric.

Eric looked around.

"What's this girl even talking about," he thought to himself.

"Erhm. It's a car. Who knocks when entering a car? This doesn't make any sense." Eric said

"Which part?" Beatrice asked

"The part where you and your sister are going after each other because of a certain guy. The knocking on the car part too. Makes no sense."

"First of all, he is not just a guy. Secondly, I don't know, and I don't care what my sister has said. Get him out of that ray hole." Beatrice commanded.

"I am not your puppet okay? I am not just a guy who gets things done for you. I am a lawyer, not a crook." Eric was getting upset.

"You are my mother's spokesperson and an integral member of the VPC communication team. You're Mrs.

Nimako's confidant. Mention a more criminal position... I will wait." Beatrice pointed out.

Eric processed it. There was nothing he could say.

"You know I don't understand this madness with Nkrumah," Eric complained.

"Let me summarize for you then. Nkrumah, the man you don't rate has information that will end us. All of us. Me, you, everyone. Because those documents are proved to all the accusations against us that cannot be proved. Three generations of my family have been looking for those documents. I intend to be the last. That's how important this is to me." Beatrice revealed.

"Kill him then. Isn't that how you deal with threats?" Eric suggested.

"You kill him and you live the rest of your life looking over your shoulder, not knowing where that information could be roaming. You find it and that's liberation." Beatrice explained.

"Huhn. Makes sense now." Eric said.

"Good. Now that you understand. Get out of my car and go get him out of there. And please, knock the next time you are entering my car." Beatrice warned.

"Truth is, only your mother can get him out of there. The place is a property of the underworld. Only the inner circle has authority. What I can do is make a good case to your mother, and with your support, we can get him out of there... Hopefully, get him to talk." Eric explained.

"Good. Do that." Beatrice said.

Eric left the car. Beatrice put the music back on and she wasn't even in the mood to sing anymore. She rolled her eyes and drove off.

*****

Another beautiful day was born in the private prison facility. The gym equipment was spread out all over the room. A guard stood at the gate monitoring them. A few other inmates were there too. They often had this gym session to keep them fit.

Nkrumah tried to raise dumbbells. He was not having it easy as the bruises from the beatings he got the last time were still with him. Kwame was sweating on the treadmill. He went at it a while and then came down, panting. He came to sit on the empty seat beside where Nkrumah was.

"You are a hell of a fighter boy, look at you, back on your feet," Kwame said.

Nkrumah was concentrating, slowly he went up and then down.

"Do you miss home?" Nkrumah asked Kwame.

Kwame giggles…

"If you had the slightest idea how quickly people forget the dead. I have been here for six years if I am not mistaken. They staged an accident. I died in that accident. To everyone else I am dead. Six years is a long time to hold onto a memory of a dead man... You miss home don't you?" Kwame asked.

"I do. I can only imagine what she is going through. She is the reason I am holding on. Perhaps, just perhaps I will get to hold her hands again." Nkrumah strengthened himself.

Kwame rubbed Nkrumah's shoulder. He understood and he deeply sympathized.

"You remember when I told you I have a special feeling about you?... I have an idea. I need you to trust me… Do you trust me?"

Nkrumah looked at him for a very long time and then slowly nodded. Kwame nodded back as they both looked at each other with a sense of hope.

"Hey, guard! I think my friend here has something to tell you." Kwame called out.

"No talking mate. Shush it." The guard warned.

"You would want to hear this…" Kwame convinced.

The guard approached them.

"Don't waste my time mate. What is it?" The guard asked.

"Go ahead, say it," Kwame said to Nkrumah.

Nkrumah looked confused. He was confused. He was very aware Kwame was up to something but whatever it was he had no idea.

"Tell him or I will," Kwame said.

"Okay. What is going on here?" The guard grew curious.

Night fell in the cells. Kwame was a happy man. He couldn't hide his joy as he paced up and down the cell room. Nkrumah was in his bed, keeping his calm and doing the reading this time.

"He fell for it. I can't believe he did. Oh God. This is so refreshing." Kwame said, and excited!

"Your plan will only get me out of here. What happens to you?" Nkrumah asked.

Kwame smiled at Nkrumah. A man who knew what he was doing. He was so focused. He knew something good would be born.

"You getting out of here will only be the beginning of the plan. Nobody has ever come here and left breathing. You have no idea how long I have been waiting, praying, and hoping for this day." Kwame happily said.

He went to his bed and then pulled out a small piece of paper that he had hidden for a long time.

"I heard rumors about this place. And I knew going after the VPC meant I was destined to end up here. So, before I came here, I planted a tracker in my arm. I had to deactivate it to pass security. Here is the code." Kwame revealed.

He handed the little paper to Nkrumah who was still trying to process everything Kwame was saying.

"When you hopefully get out. find an IT person and activate it. The guy who gave it to me said it can last up to fifteen years. I can only hope he wasn't lying. If you can locate me from the outside, our mission will be complete. Because everybody in this hole is evidence of how corrupt the VPC and all their other African counterparts are. We have a chance to end the network of corruption that is widespread across the continent. Every day that passes they become more powerful. This is our chance, and you are the beginning." Kwame said.

A few days later, Kwame was in his bed, facing the dirty ceiling up above. A guard escorted Nkrumah into the cell. Nkrumah was not in the usual uniform. He had been fitted into a plain white shirt and an oversized pair of shorts.

"Privacy?... Please." Nkrumah asked the guard.

The guard put that into contemplation. But he finally agreed.

"You have two minutes."

He said after a while of thinking. He closed the door and left the two alone. Kwame came out of the bed and hugged Nkrumah tightly. An emotional moment that was.

"Thank you for everything," Nkrumah said.

"No. Thank you. For giving me something to hold on to." Kwame replied in appreciation.

"I have always wanted to ask. Why didn't they just kill you people?" Nkrumah asked.

"Intelligent question. Because they find us still helpful. We work for them now."

"I will come for you," Nkrumah assured.

"I know you will boy, I know you will. Congratulations on being the first man to walk out of here alive." Kwame happily said.

"Write that somewhere so people don't forget. Nkrumah said playfully.

"Remember everything we talked about. Redemption has started. And you boy will lead us to that promised land." Kwame reminded Nkrumah.

They shared a very affectionate smile as they looked at each other. The guard came back in shortly.

"Alright time to go. Come on, move it." The guard said.

Nkrumah stretched his hand for a handshake. Kwame placed a firm one in. They followed it with a man hug and Nkrumah left. Both men were teary, but they kept it together.

Chapter 7

Eric sat on the bonnet of his car under a bridge. He was speaking into his air pods as he looked to be on a call.

"No. Hell no. Don't permit them. Don't grant any interviews to foreign media. Let them mind their business, let us mind ours." Eric spoke on the phone.

A van was coming towards him.

"Hold on. Let me get back to you." Eric said and ended the call. He stood up as the Van came to the park. A masked man came out of the driving seat. Another one accompanied him.

"Hey. Unbelievable. You are hiding your faces from me." Eric said.

But they didn't say a word. They opened the back of the van where Nkrumah sat with a sack over his head and his hands tied at his back. They threw him onto the ground as if he was a bag of rice and then off, they went. Eric went to Nkrumah and then got rid of the sack.

"We meet again," Eric said.

Moments later. Nkrumah was in the car with Eric who was driving. Nkrumah at the moment was enjoying a piece of a roasted corn. He hadn't had good food in a long time. The quiet went on for a while, and then they found themselves in traffic. Eric broke the silence.

"Just a recap. I know I have mentioned it a million times. But no one can know what happened."

"Eric? that's the name, right?" Nkrumah asked.

"Yeah. Eric." Eric replied.

"Who do you work for?" Nkrumah inquired.

"Erhm... Well, I am the guy who got you out of the prison so the answer should be obvious." Eric said.

"Do you work for the VPC?" Nkrumah asked.

The question put Eric on the edge.

"No. I work for you, but I answer to them." Eric replied.

"So, you people put me in jail and one of you is my lawyer."

"Okay. This will be the last time you say something like that. When you say this anywhere else you will be arrested for treason. And there is nothing I will be able to do to help you. The VPC had nothing to do with this." Eric warned.

The traffic started to move.

"So how do you explain all of these? Why was I in a VPC rat hole? Why are you helping me? Nkrumah asked.

"God. Who is feeding you with all these information? The VPC doesn't have a rat hole. You were in a private detention facility which is one hundred percent legal. And I am helping you because your wife, or fiancee, or whatever she is to you paid me good money to get you out of there." Eric said.

"You didn't get me out of there. The only reason I am here is because I told the guards that I can find the treasure box which may contain the documents."

The car slowly came to a stop in front of a house. That was Nkrumah's house.

"It's a box and some piece of papers. Nkrumah. It's not worth more than your life or the life of the people you care about. Whoever these people are, they have proven how powerful and influential they can be. The scary part is they are anonymous. That means they could be anybody." Eric advised.

"Including the VPC?" Nkrumah asked.

Eric sighed. After a long pause...

"Including the VPC... Nkrumah if you know anything at all, you can come to me. You can trust me. But if you don't tell them what they want, they won't stop coming after you. And there will be nothing any of us can do about it."

Nkrumah smiled sarcastically.

"Thanks for the ride. But you are not my lawyer. You're a liar." Nkrumah said.

He stepped out of the car and walked into the house... Eric made a call.

"Keep eyes on him. Follow him everywhere. I think he knows something." Eric said to someone on the phone.

*****

Nkrumah walked up to his front door. Sighed a big relief. He had been waiting for this moment for a very long time. The house was a middle-class type of home. Nothing fancy. It had a fairly big compound and a portion of it had beautiful green grass. He knocked. And guess who... Beatrice. Nkrumah's long-time girlfriend turned wife was Beatrice. At his sight, she at once broke into tears.

"Oh my God, Nkrumah." Beatrice cried.

She put in a very tight hug, followed by a passionate kiss.

"I thought I was never going to see you." She said.

"I am here baby. It's fine…" Nkrumah consoled her.

He rubbed his hand on her back as he hugged his crying girl. They broke from the long hug and went into their room.

"Are you hungry, have you eaten," Beatrice asked.

"I am fine. Calm down. It's me, I am here." Nkrumah calmed her down.

Beatrice nodded and wiped off the tears on her face.

On the same night, Nkrumah and Beatrice were eating dinner at their table. The place was quiet. Only the sound of the cutlery was heard. There was this awkwardness to the whole thing. Beatrice broke the uncomfortable silence.

"You've been quiet since you came back. Anything you will want to talk about?" Beatrice asked.

Nkrumah took his time, in no rush at all to answer.

"I am fine." He said after a while.

"You don't look fine. It's me. Talk to me. What's on your mind?" Beatrice asked again.

Nkrumah took a deep breath. Looked into the eyes of Beatrice and smiled.

"Questions," Nkrumah said.

Beatrice was excited.

"There we go. Let's hear it." She said.

"Did you know?" That was an unexpected and straight question by Nkrumah.

"Know what?" Beatrice asked puzzled.

"Did you know that all those anonymous letters, and all the interviews of mine that got canceled? All the threats and warnings, did you know it was your mother and her stupid party?"

"No. I won't let you insult my mother. And what are you talking about?" Beatrice charged.

"Oh please, don't play the ignorant card. You know what I am talking about." Nkrumah said.

Beatrice slowly got teary. One cry-baby she was.

"Nkrumah, where is this coming from?" Beatrice asked.

"Is this even real? Is any of these real... Do you like me at all?" Nkrumah asked.

At that point, the tears were running down her face.

"I love you." She said.

"Or you are spying on me for your mother," Nkrumah asked.

"What have they done to you? What have they done to my Nkrumah…" Beatrice cried.

"I don't know but I will find out. And for your sake baby. I hope you are telling me the truth. I love you; I do. But if I find out any of this is a conspiracy, you are going to see a side of me you've never seen." Nkrumah promised her.

He stood from the table and headed out. Beatrice followed him.

"We need to talk." Beatrice cried out.

"It can wait," Nkrumah replied and walked off.

Beatrice hit her hand on the table in frustration. She entered into deep thought.

*****

Shadows had shortened. The sun was still in the sky emitting its powerful rays. At the provision shop, a senior citizen was the attendant at the shop. He was attending to a girl buying a pack of soap. Kweku Asante was in the queue. He had a baseball cap on, and a hoodie too. Desperately trying to be unnoticed. The girl finished and left.

"What do you want son." The attendant asked.

"A pack of sachet water," Kweku responded.

The man looked at Kweku Asante carefully. Kweku on the other hand, trying hard not to make eye contact. The attendant brought out the pack of water and handed it to him.

"Ten cedis please." The attendant mentioned.

Kweku paid and waited for his change.

"You did the right thing. We are all tired." The attendant said.

"Sorry?" Kweku acted ignorant.

"On your show. Calling them out. They closed the station you know." The attendant asked.

"Sorry, I don't know what you are talking about." Kweku pretended.

He took his change, picked up the bag, and briskly walked off.

The night had approached. A small motel facility on the outskirts of town, very small, out of shape, and isolated. Most of the things in the room were from a long time. It was as if nobody even used the room anymore. The bed was a little rusted. Cobwebs hung in corners. The carpet on the floor had all sorts of stains. But that was where Kweku was.

He was watching a very old CRT television when he heard a knock on the door. He reached under his pillow and pulled out a pistol. He carefully walked towards the door, scared.

"Who is there?" Kweku asked.

"You ordered food." That was a girl's voice

Kweku sighed and lowered the pistol. He brought out his wallet and took out some money. He then opened the door and quickly did the exchange all while looking down and acting weird just so he wasn't recognized. He came inside with his pack of food. He put the pistol back under the pillow.

Nkrumah had a small backpack on the bed. He was packing a few pieces of clothing into it. Beatrice walked in shortly, all hyped and excited. Her excitement immediately vanished from her face as she saw Nkrumah packing.

"Oh. I - was planning to serve you breakfast in bed." Beatrice said romantically. Nkrumah said nothing in return. He was just packing.

"Can you at least tell me where you are going?" Beatrice asked.

"I am going home," Nkrumah responded.

"This is your home." Beatrice was confused.

"Hometown. I am going to my hometown." Nkrumah cleared her thoughts.

"What? you got home like three days ago."

Nkrumah didn't say anything. He put his last pieces into the bag.

"Are you punishing me? Because this silent treatment is breaking my heart. I have been seated in this bed every night alone, praying and wishing you would come back safe. I got you the best lawyer I know. And you come back, and this is what I get?" Beatrice complained.

"You didn't do anything wrong Beatrice. I just don't want you anywhere around what I am about to do. It could be dangerous." Nkrumah explained.

"Can we at least talk? There are things I have to tell you." Beatrice said.

Nkrumah went to her and held her face as he looked into her eyes.

"Hey. I will be back. I promise. I just need to get this done. For all our good, okay. Continue praying for me. Can you do that for me?"

Beatrice nodded continuously.

"Thank you." Nkrumah appreciated and kissed her lips gently.

"And can you please tell nobody where I am headed?" Nkrumah pleaded.

"Fine," Beatrice assured.

"Thank you. Come here."

Nkrumah hugged her one last time and he left. Beatrice walked to the bed and threw herself into it. She picked a pillow, covered her face, and screamed... She afterward hit her face with the pillow as she talked. "What - am I – doing!"

*****

A very busy station. Public transport systems mentioned different locations as conductors also loaded their various cars to their various destinations. Cars went to and fro. Same with humans. Nkrumah was part of the people there. He was spotted asking one of the conductors something. He pointed in a direction.

Nkrumah was seated in an old ritiki troski. The driver started the engine and drove them out of the station. Nkrumah who was at the window side of the troski had his nose covered to protect himself from all the dust they were traveling through.

Nkrumah arrived at his destination. He was in Agona Bobikuma. He went by a few people who went to and from the stream. This stream was called "Awommerew," meaning, "easy birth delivery." It was believed that any pregnant woman who drank from the stream delivered easily without any difficulty during childbirth.

A hunter also had his game on his shoulder as he headed home. Nkrumah looked around at the place of his birth. Where he hadn't been in a long time. He was still asking people for information. He asked one, two, three people. They all shook their heads and were not of help. He asked a few people, Still. Then he met a woman, he asked her, and he was directed.

A small house is situated on the farm. Nkrumah got to the house and knocked on the door. A boy, Seth came to the door. Seth was in his late teens.

"Hi, Sorry. I am looking for one Mr. Paul." Nkrumah asked.

Seth looked completely astonished. His surprised face slowly turned into a warm welcoming smile.

"Welcome… We have been waiting for you. Please, come in." Seth said as he welcomed Nkrumah.

Inside the room, Mr. Paul sat on a mat with his back leaning on the wall for support. He was very old and dying. He was stiff and sat upright like a statue. Mr. Paul wore a key on his neck.

"Grandpa. Your visitor has come." Seth notified Mr. Paul

"This is him? Can he talk?" Nkrumah asked as he was puzzled.

"Say hi. Introduce yourself." Seth told Nkrumah.

"Hi. Mr. Paul. My name is Nkrumah. Kwame lots is my friend. He asked me to come and look for you. He said you have something to tell me."

Nkrumah waited for a response, but Mr. Paul didn't even move.

"I am sorry. Does he - speak?" Nkrumah asked Seth.

"What is it you want to know," Seth asked.

It was evening. A small bonfire in the middle of the thick woods. Nkrumah and Seth sat around the fire on logs.

"He never stopped talking about you. Everyone called him crazy, but he believed the ancestors would bring you to him. He told me point blank that he won't die until he gives you the key. He believes that is his quest." Seth said.

"He told you what happened to my dad?" Nkrumah asked.

"Yes, he did... He said a few minutes before the murder, your parents were working on their farm laughing and chitchatting when he strolled by. He waved at them to greet and they waved back. On his way, he stopped in his tracks at once because he forgot something. He contemplated whether or not to go back. He then turned back, a few steps in and he decided again it was not worth it. He went in the direction he was traveling earlier but no; something just wouldn't let him. He then decided to go back for whatever it was he forgot. He said he was almost at the same spot he saw your parents when he noticed something unusual. Two muscled men, each stood behind your mother and father. Then there was a woman who stood in front of your parents who were kneeling. The woman talked angrily at them. He said he found a suitable spot to hide as he watched the whole scene. The woman pointed fingers and issued all sorts of threats but neither your father nor mother said a word. They both kept their mouth, shivered to death." Seth narrated.

"He said the woman then issued the command to execute them. The two men brought out knives and stabbed them, in no particular fashion. They left them there and hurried off. They made sure they weren't detected. When the armed people were finally out of sight, he rushed onto the scene where he found your father still breathing. The key hung around your father's neck. He said he noticed that your father wanted to speak so he leaned in to hear him. He said the exact words of your father were, "*Take the key, find my son. He will know what to do with it.*" Seth added.

Nkrumah had been reminded of his pain. Tears flowed down his cheeks.

"Did he see them? Did he see who did this to my family?"

"None that he mentioned. But he said they left in big black cars."

Seth replies stroke Nkrumah. He then stared into the fire as he went deep into his thoughts.

A throwback of young Nkrumah, who spotted a car that came toward him. He remembered an important detail. The face of the woman she waved at. It was the face of Mrs. Nimako who was younger then, but her tribal marks were very visible.

Nkrumah looked to have figured out who killed his parents. Even with a face filled with tears, his eyes lit up with the thirst for revenge. His jawbone showed, obviously he had been triggered. He cracked his fingers with an evil run through his mind.

"You can stay at our place if you have nowhere to be," Seth suggested.

"Thank you. I appreciate." Nkrumah replied.

The following morning, Nkrumah stood in front of the abandoned house. He gently soaked in the memories the place came with. It was obvious nobody had been there in a long time. Hanged on his neck was the key-made necklace. It was finally in his possession.

He stepped into the house. Dusts all over. Cobwebs. Rats and cockroaches had made the room their playground. Nkrumah looked around, clueless.

"Come on. What do I have to do?" He said to himself.

He played with the key as he looked around and tried to find something that would at least trigger a memory.

His eyes landed on his father's rifle. He stared at it and smiled.

Nkrumah remembered his father, seated outside. The key-made necklace around his father's neck, cleaning that exact rifle. A young Nkrumah, about ten years old sat there watching his father.

"Papa. My friends say that anyone whose father does not own a car or a big house as those in the city own is poor." Young Nkrumah told his father.

His father chuckled and replied...

"Your friends know nothing. Riches are not measured in cars or houses. Riches are measured in the impact your life has on other lives. You are only as rich as the positive influence you make on people."

"Does that mean you are rich?" Young Nkrumah asked his father.

"Yes, your father is the richest man in this village. You see this..." His father pointed to the key.

"It holds a secret wanted by many. That is why we have to keep a low profile. If not for that, we would be rich enough to buy all this village and even more." His father revealed.

"I want us to buy this village so I can go hunting anywhere I want." Young Nkrumah said.

"Riches fade, my son. No matter how much. But a rich soul is worth a million dozen bars of gold. Come, let me show you how to hold a rifle."

Nkrumah run into the arms of his seated father. He made himself comfortable on his father's lap. Nkrumah's father put the rifle in his hands and helped him aim. Then slowly he let go. He left Nkrumah to hold the gun. Nkrumah fidgeted as the gun was slightly heavier but managed to keep his cool.

"Our lives as men are like this gun. You always have the option to pull the trigger or keep your bullet for another day's fight. I am keeping mine." He said and took the gun from Nkrumah.

He then pointed into the distance at a tree view.

"You see that tree there? One day, you will stand in front of it and make the biggest decision of your life. I have made mine. You see this…"

He took off the key and put it in Nkrumah's hand.

"Everything you need in life is in your hand. We are wanted men, Nkrumah, and one day you will decide whether to stay in hiding like I have or take the fight to the oppressors." His father said.

Nkrumah looked at the key in his hand.

His flashback ended, as he looked in his hand holding the key. Everything made sense now. He understood all that his father had revealed to him. He grabbed a shovel and then marched urgently out to the woods.

Nkrumah came to the tree his father pointed at him when he was little. He began to dig. The first hole, no luck. He went again. Another hole no luck. Nkrumah was not a man who would give in that easily. He tried a third, the same as the other two. Then again, and again.

He hit the shovel against the tree angrily as he screamed out his frustration. The bark of the tree on the side he hit slipped. And he noticed. That was not usual. He went closer and saw that that part of the tree had been glued onto it. It was old, so peeling it was easy. He peeled off that portion of the tree and what he found amazed him. A rusty old metal case.

He pulled it out. Found the lock. Used the key on his neck to open it. He found about eight gold stones. His jaw dropped. Eyes wide opened. Unreal. He wiped his face with his hands, just to make sure all of that was happening. He lifted the gold bars and he found the papers. A lot of them bonded together with hand stitches. Nkrumah was shocked to the core.

"Holy mother of God." He exclaimed.

He heard the sound of a gun load.

"Drop it. Hands up. And walk away." That was a male voice.

Nkrumah slowly raised his hands, stood in front of the treasure, and then slowly turned. He saw the man. Thick tall bearded assassin. The bald head had a burn on his face. A very scary-looking dude.

"Who sent you?" Nkrumah asked.

"None of your business. I am about to send you... To your grave." The assassin said.

"We can talk about this. You can take whatever they asked you to come for and leave. I don't want any of these." Nkrumah said.

"Those aren't my orders."

"Who ordered you?... The VPC? Who? Anything they are offering you I can offer double." He lured the assassin.

"You are talking too much."

"I want a fair fight. Give me the chance to go down like a man."

"Hey. Shut up. What do you think this is? Spartans? Move away from the treasure... I don't want blood over it." The assassin warned.

"Make me..." Nkrumah was talking when the assassin overlapped.

"Hey, you're testing my patience!"

The assassin who slowly loosed his calm charged toward Nkrumah.

"Yes, I dare you." Nkrumah dared the assassin.

The assassin reached Nkrumah and then shoved him off. Nkrumah skillfully held onto his strong firm hand and used his legs to kick the gun from his other hand.

"Come on. Fight me." Nkrumah dared him.

The assassin who felt embarrassed and humiliated tore his singlet and moved toward Nkrumah. He threw a heavy right punch. Nkrumah ducked and put one into his right ribs. The giant didn't even feel tickled. He grabbed Nkrumah by the neck and raised him. Nkrumah's legs hanged.

"How dare you?" The assassin said.

Nkrumah punched into his groin and he let go of him immediately. He struggled to catch his breath and then ran to pick up the pistol that the assassin dropped. He aimed and shot, but no fire. Again, and again. Still, nothing.

"If that gun was loaded, I would have shot you as soon as I found you. I didn't have plans to kill you. But that just changed. I always wondered what Akosua wanted with you anyway." The assassin said.

He charged toward Nkrumah, a step, then two. As soon as he took the third one...

"Pooh!" A shot was fired from a distance. Straight into the head of the giant assassin. He fell like a tree to the ground, his brain all over. Nkrumah looked around. Shivering and panting. He was looking for where the shot came from then he saw Seth, holding a shotgun running toward him.

"Are you okay?" Seth asked.

Nkrumah nodded and panted heavily, eyes wide open and sweating.

Some moments later, they were in Mr. Paul's house. Nkrumah knelt before Paul who was not getting any better. Seth stood by, in what looked to be an emotional goodbye.

"I don't know if you can hear me, but I wanted to say thank you... For waiting, for holding on, for believing that I will show up. I am sorry that it took this long, but I'm here now. And because of you, life is about to get a whole lot better for all of us. You are lucky to have a grandson like

Seth. More than lucky. I really don't know how to express how I am feeling in words. But I want you to know that I appreciate everything you've done."

"Now he can rest in peace," Seth said.

Nkrumah came to his feet and went to hug Seth warmly.

"When you finish taking care of your papa. Come to the city." Nkrumah told Seth.

He handed a paper with his number on there to him.

"And call me. There is always a place in my house for you." Nkrumah added.

"Just like there is for you here," Seth responded and they hugged again.

C h a p t e r 9

It was another beautiful day in a Catholic temple. Abigail's heel echoed through the empty church room. She modeled her way into the confession booth.

"I got your text. What do you want this time?" Abigail asked Selas.

"Ah yes. I was wondering when you will show up." Selas said.

"I am late for a meeting," Abigail stressed.

"Well then. I won't waste your time. My bosses have decided to step things up."

"What is that supposed to mean?" Abigail asked.

"It means, things are speeding. And so, must you." Selas explained.

"I have told you everything I already know," Abigail confessed.

"And I am very grateful. On your way out of here, you will see an envelope of cash. My bosses want you to know that they appreciate your service. You will also find a bug that you will plant in your mother's study room."

"Are you out of your mind?"

"We all are Abigail."

"You promised me a written agreement," Abigail asked.

"I am working on that," Selas replied.

"I don't believe you. I don't trust you will leave my family out of this. I think you will do anything you can to destroy the party. Even if it means destroying us."

"Well, then we have to make sure it doesn't come to that. I thought you said you were late for a meeting. Shouldn't you be going?"

Abigail rolled her eyes.

"Unbelievable." She said to herself.

"Oh. And before you go you might check your mail. I sent you another video you will be very happy to see. I see you have a thing for small boys." Selas teased.

Abigail stormed out. Angry at herself. Just like Selas said there was a small bug and an envelope of cash. She snatched both and continued her walk off. Her heels still echoed as she walked briskly out.

*****

Nkrumah marched into the hall straight face and not happy. Shouting, behind him is Beatrice.

"I am talking to you and you walk out on me..." Beatrice complained.

Nkrumah who was yards ahead of Beatrice got seated in time and turned on the television. Completely ignoring his wife's whinnying. Beatrice finally got to the hall, completely outraged. She went straight to the television and turned it off. She then stood in front of the television, arms folded.

"I have had enough okay? I am tired. You came back from jail and we never had our moments. You left for your village, I am here thinking you will catch your sanity once you are back and here you are even more sneaky and secretive than you were before. I am your wife for crying out loud. We need to have a conversation. I have a body that is starving for sex."

Nkrumah was calm and comported.

"Please, hand me the remote. I just want to watch television." He said.

"Not going to happen. What is wrong with you? Who is this man? I need my Nkrumah back." Beatrice said.

Yes! And just like that, Nkrumah also switched gears. He stood and faced her squarely.

"Do you...? Maybe you should tell that to your psycho mother who sent men after me to kill me. And maybe you should tell that crazy party of yours who threw me behind bars for no reason. If you want your Nkrumah back, go and get him from them. Your parent and your so-called dirty legacy of a party." Nkrumah charged.

Beatrice was crying at this point. Honestly, she had no clue what Nkrumah was saying.

"What are you talking about?" Beatrice cried.

"Oh please! Wipe those crocodile tears. I am sick and tired of you crying your way out of everything. You knew about this. Look in my eyes and tell me that anything I am saying is new to you. You are a big fraud. But why am I even surprised... The fruit does not fall far away from the tree."

"Nkrumah," Beatrice called as she cried.

"Look at me. Look into my eyes and tell me you didn't know all along that all those anonymous threats were from your people." Nkrumah said.

Nkrumah closed the gap. Looked into the crying eyes of Beatrice with nothing but rage and anger in his eyes. Beatrice said nothing. She just cried. A few seconds passed.

"I thought as much. But your end is coming. Trust me. I will deal with you and every single corrupt member of that smelling party. And as for your mother who killed my parents and tried to kill me. Tell her that no amount of guards can save her from what I have installed for her. I will have my revenge." Nkrumah threatened.

He turned. He began to walk away. Two steps in and then...

"I am pregnant," Beatrice said.

Nkrumah stopped at his pace. Rooted to the spot.

"I am carrying your baby Nkrumah. I love you."

Nkrumah then turned to look at the innocent teary face of Beatrice. He took a long look but didn't say a word. He continued his journey out of the hall and left Beatrice to her sad thoughts.

*****

The sun had already vanished from the sky. It was evening. The air was very cold outside. Mrs. Nimako was seated on her little throne in her study room watching a documentary on her personal computer. Abigail walked in not long after looking intimidated.

"Mom," Abigail called.

Mrs. Nimako paused the film.

"Baby girl. What is it? Why do you look like someone stole your toys?"

Abigail came to sit down. She made no eye contact at all.

"You remember when you said you will forgive us no matter what we do as long as we come clean to you. Did you mean that, or it was another political talk?" Abigail tried to verify.

"Of course, I mean that. You are my daughter." Mrs. Nimako confirmed.

"I did something, Mom. Something... terrible," Abigail said.

"It's okay. Don't worry. You can talk to me."

"There is this private investigator who approached me, and I accepted to work with him."

"Wait. What?"

"Mom, it wasn't willing. He had something on me. He blackmailed me into helping him."

"And by what help do you mean?" Mrs. Nimako asked.

"He wanted me to be his insider over here and feed him with information," Abigail revealed.

"Wow. Just, wow." Mrs. Nimako said and nodded her head continuously.

"I swear I didn't tell him anything useful and now he wants me to plant a bug in your office."

"You got to be kidding me." Mrs. Nimako said.

"I know. That's why I am here. I thought I could handle this on my own, but I can't. Mom, he has something that can ruin me. My reputation will go as far as messing with your political career. You need to help me stop him." Abigail pleaded.

"This investigator. What is his name?"

"Selas." Abigail replied.

"And how long have you two been in contact?" Mrs. Nimako asked.

"About three weeks."

"Three weeks! Abigail three weeks and you are now coming to me?" Mrs. Nimako got upset.

"I am sorry. I didn't know what to do." Abigail apologized.

Mrs. Nimako went quiet for a while. She reflected on a possible next move while Abigail sat in the glory of her shame.

"Have you not learned anything?" Mrs. Nimako asked.

"I didn't tell him anything I promise. I was just leading him on, so he doesn't leak those videos." Abigail explained.

"It's fine. Don't worry. I will take care of him. Stop talking to him. That's an order."

"Yes, Mom... I love you, Mom."

Mrs. Nimako rolled her eyes. "Get some rest, Abigail."

*****

It was around 11 am. Kweku Asante was walking home. He held a rubber full of toiletries. As usual, he was dressed in a disguise and the hoodie over the head was what he hid his face.

Kweku Asante paced quickly, head down, and tried his best to avoid any contact at all even though the road was fairly empty and quiet. He instinctively picked up weird vibes and stopped in his tracks. Something was not right, and he felt it.

Kweku took a rather unusual turn as he felt he was being followed. That took him into a part of the town that appeared to be a slum. It had a ghetto-ish feel and had corners all over. Ideal place for evasion.

Nkrumah also tried his best to blend with the darkness as he followed Kweku from quite a distance. He got to the turn and used the exact turn Kweku used. A few steps in and he receives a text. He reached for his phone, bowed his head to read and from nowhere, a knife was on his throat. Kweku had Nkrumah's back against his chest with his little pocketknife right on his throat. The slightest mistake and Nkrumah was a dead man.

"It will be in your best interest if you don't make any unnecessary movements." Kweku cautioned.

"I come in peace," Nkrumah said.

"You will be leaving in pieces. Who sent you? Why are you following me?" Kweku asked.

Nkrumah was panting, so scared that he could barely speak well.

"To - to..." Nkrumah stammered.

"Open your mouth and speak," Kweku said.

Nkrumah took in deep breath and got his speech under control.

"To - to strike for the perfection of character... To defend the part of truth." Nkrumah said fumbling.

Kweku slowly loosened up as he listened to Nkrumah.

"To honor the spirit of etiquette," Nkrumah concluded.

Kweku let's go of Nkrumah completely. Whatever those words were, they sure meant a lot to him and his reaction showed that. Nkrumah still had his hands up even though he had been let go off. He slowly turned to face Kweku.

"I come in peace. I just want to talk." Nkrumah clarified.

A few moments later, Nkrumah was seated on a bed in the motel where Kweku hid. Kweku paced up and down the room in uncertainty.

"How did you find me? Who else knows I am here? What do you want from me?" Kweku asked.

"Bro, bro relax. It's just us. Nobody knows your whereabouts; nobody knows I am here with you." Nkrumah said.

"But how? How did Mrs. Morrison just give out my location to a stranger," Kweku said.

"Because I recited the same lines, I recited to you that got me in here. And I told her the same thing I am about to tell you... I had time with your mentor. Kwame Lots. Before I left, we drew a plan. A plan that has the same goal you have. To expose the VPC for who they are and end the rule of the wicked. He asked me to find you and said I could trust you. You were part of his plan, Kweku. For his sake, help me." Nkrumah detailed.

Kweku Asante at that point had given Nkrumah his hundred percent attention.

"Go on," Kweku said.

"We didn't know you would be on the government's wanted list so fast. This will mess with the plan a little. But I have a plan B… We need to find Kwame Lots. He is alive, together with all the other officials who spoke up or criticized this government. All of them." Nkrumah revealed.

Kweku's eyes lit up with hope.

"Kwame Lots is alive?" Kweku asked.

"Very alive and waiting for us," Nkrumah said.

"How can I help? What do I have to do?"

"We need an IT personnel. One that is willing to break the rules. Someone who knows the internet. Who can buy and sell almost anything undetected." Nkrumah explained.

"You have come to the right man. I know just the person. Naruto." Kweku said.

*****

Naruto was in her early twenties. A girl with a sassy badass vibe. Her short hair was dyed gold. Her arms were covered in tattoos and she had a lot of piercings on her ear and face. Nkrumah found Naruto in a car garage on the following day.

"Are you Naruto?" Nkrumah asked.

"Yes. You're looking at me." Naruto said.

"I need your help." Nkrumah begged.

"Of course, you do. That's why I am here. What kind of car do you want to rent? We have a wide range. The good news is we have partner shops all across so even if the car you want is not here, we can still get it for you. Cool, right?" Naruto explained.

Nkrumah cleared his throat.

"Monkey, crocodile, lizard, bananas," Nkrumah said in an undertone.

Naruto became alarmed.

"How did he know all these..." Naruto thought to herself.

"Bro. What the fuck?" Naruto asked.

"Sorry. Kweku said if I said that you will understand." Nkrumah mentioned.

"Hell yeah, I will. How about you go tell Kweku to go fuck himself." Naruto said.

"Okay, okay. That is harsh. Kweku is in trouble."

"Good. I pray he dies. Son of a bitch fucked me and left me for good. I know I look tough, but I am not. I feel for that bastard and he broke my heart." Naruto poured out her anger.

Naruto was emotionally angrier. She turned to walk away.

"Peanut butter," Nkrumah said.

Naruto stopped and turned slowly.

"He told me to say that when it ever got this. He didn't break your heart. He just got into serious trouble. How about, I tell you I can take you to him." Nkrumah said convincingly.

Nkrumah and Naruto sneaked their way up to Kweku's hiding place. They knocked and Kweku quickly let them in.

"Did anyone see you coming in here?" Kweku asked.

"No. You have to calm down. I know how this works." Nkrumah said as Naruto looked away.

"Hi," Kweku said to Naruto.

Naruto at that point looked at him. A long while. Then matched straight to him and slapped him. A heavy slap that was.

"I deserve that. I miss you. Can I kiss you?" Kweku asked

"I thought you would never ask," Naruto replied.

Naruto dropped her bag onto the ground, ran toward Kweku, and hugged him with his legs wrapped around his waist. Hands over his neck and lips locked. They took the action onto the bed. Nkrumah stood by, pretended not to see what was going on. But they were overdoing it. He cleared his throat, and…

"Guys," Nkrumah called.

They didn't mind him. They were busy having fun, kissed, and smooched noisily. It was just an annoying sight.

"Guys!" Nkrumah yelled.

They both sat up and wore innocent faces. Like two children whose dad just caught them in an act.

"Time is not our friend. There will be more than enough time to finish whatever you are doing. But please can we get to work." Nkrumah said.

"Oh, sure. What do you want?" Naruto asked.

"An army... And I need you to sell some very precious stuff online. Can you do that and still keep us anonymous?" Nkrumah replied and asked.

"Please. Don't insult me. I can sell this country overnight and no one will trace it back to me." Naruto bragged.

"That's not a bluff. She can." Kweku said.

"Well then. Let's get to it." Nkrumah said.

*****

The moon had already settled in the sky. Selas was seated on the bonnet of his car, smoking. Abigail drove on and came to park her car. She stepped out.

"You can't be doing this in public," Abigail said.

She snatched the cigarette from Selas and threw it onto the ground. She then stepped on it to kill the fire.

"Really?" Selas asked.

"Say what you need to say and get the hell out of here," Abigail said.

"I see you have finally found your balls. Impressive! Get in the car. The boss wants to meet you." Selas said.

Selas stood from the bonnet and approached the driver's seat of the car.

"Come on," Selas called Abigail.

"And if I don't?" Abigail asked.

"Trust me, baby, you wouldn't want to know." Selas warned Abigail.

Selas went to sit in the car. Honks at Abigail who looked to be in two minds. She joined Selas in the car and they drove off.

Moments later, they got to an isolated part of the town. Selas's car throttled to a stop in what looked to be the middle of nowhere. Another black car with tinted glasses was also parked at the place.

"We are here," Selas said.

Abigail looked around. And immediately on edge, everything was off. She began to wonder if she had walked herself into a trap.

"Where is this?" Abigail asked.

"I told you we are here to see the boss," Selas replied

"I heard what you said. But where is this?" Abigail asked again.

"Come on. We don't have time for questions and answers. Come down and act normal." Selas suggested.

Selas came down from the car. Abigail followed shortly. They walked towards the other parked car.

"Smile please, it's not a funeral," Selas said.

They finally got to where the car was parked, some fifty meters away from them.

"Alright hop in," Selas said.

"Alone?" Abigail asked.

"Eerm yes. It's not a threesome." Selas replied.

Abigail walked slowly, still scared. She finally opened the car door. To her surprise, it was her mother, Mrs. Akosua Nimako.

"Mom!" Abigail said in surprise.

She hopped in. Feeling relieved just a little.

"What are you doing here? Have they kidnapped you?" Abigail asked.

"Okay, that is where I stop you. I am the boss." Mrs. Nimako said.

"Huhn? Boss. His boss?" Abigail was puzzled.

"Yes." Mrs. Nimako replied.

"Are you trying to tell me none of this is real?" Abigail asked.

"No." Mrs. Nimako replied confidently.

"All of it is made up?" Abigail asked again.

"Yes."

"So Selas? Is he not real?" Abigail verified.

"No." Mrs. Nimako replied.

"Jesus Christ, Mom."

Abigail looked away, through the tinted glass into the distance where streetlights blurred onto her sight from far away. She felt used, and to think that her own mother made all of that up was making her sick. And then it hit her.

"Wait. So, it means, you know everything," Abigail asked curiously.

"Yes." Mrs. Nimako overlapped.

"For God's sake! Mom please say something. This yes and no game isn't helping me. I am losing my mind here." Abigail said puzzling.

But Mrs. Nimako was rather relaxed and unbothered.

"I mean, what do you want me to say? In summary, I know about your senior high school lovers. And I have seen all the freaky things you do with those kids. You didn't get that from me." Mrs. Nimako said.

"So, this was a punishment?" Abigail asked.

"No. You asked to be part of the game. This was your test. Your decision-making, how you handle pressure, all of it. Abigail, this thing, it's not a gentleman's job. We are women, and it's a man's world. To be feared and respected, you need to do terrible things. You did a great job my girl, but you are not cut for something like this. And there is nothing wrong with that." Mrs. Nimako explained.

Abigail rolled her eyes.

"Yes right. It was going to be Beatrice anyway." She said.

"Abigail, I don't talk about your father enough, but he was a hell of a smart man. He cooked the books and worked the numbers. There was nothing illegal that that man couldn't change on paper. You are just like your father, Abigail. You don't need to be in the spotlight to be important. So no, I am not choosing Beatrice over you. I am giving what belongs to Caesar to Caesar." Mrs. Nimako enlightened.

Mrs. Nimako tried to touch Abigail, but she moved away from the contact.

"Well. That said. This meeting never happened. And with immediate effect, you stop seeing all those child lovers. What is wrong with you? Do you know what a reputation like that can do to you and me? Can't you find someone your age to unleash your sexual rage on?"

"You don't have to say it like that," Abigail responded unhappily.

"But I have." Mrs. Nimako replied.

"Sorry, Mom. It was a one-time thing." Abigail apologized.

"Was it? Because I have about three different videos. Abigail, we are under serious scrutiny. People want our heads. Everybody is in our business including foreign press. We don't want to do anything that will give them an advantage. We need to keep a united front. Do you understand?"

"Yes, Mom," Abigail replied and nodded.

"Good. Now ride back home with Selas. He works for you now. Whatever you see in those Senior High School boys, I pray you will see in him."

"Mom come on. You can't make jokes like that." Abigail said.

"Goodnight." Mrs. Nimako wished to Abigail.

Abigail stepped out of the car and banged the door.

It was a beautiful brand-new day. Mrs. Nimako was seated in her study room. She was on a call.

"That's fine. Yes. Mr. Johnson will make a fine candidate for attorney general. He speaks our language." Mrs. Nimako said to someone on the phone.

Beatrice entered the room like a storm.

"You promised me nothing was going to happen to him." Beatrice charged her mother, Mrs. Nimako.

Mrs. Nimako who was certainly not happy with that interruption shot back at Beatrice.

"I will have to call you back. Yes. Thank you. Bye," Mrs. Nimako said and hung up the call.

She immediately turned to Beatrice and furiously asked.

"Are you out of your mind?"

" Did you send men to kill Nkrumah?" Beatrice was so mad and charged her mother.

"It's your mother you are talking to. Kill that base in your tone or I will do that for you," Mrs. Nimako said.

"You lied to me. I am so disappointed with you and your actions," Beatrice said angrily.

"Oh please, Beatrice. You are bigger than this conversation. I did what I had to do."

"You promised me, Mother. You promised, it wasn't him you were after," Beatrice said it unhesitantly.

"That was before he became a threat to all of us." Mrs. Nimako said.

"No, I am not going to allow that. You don't have permission to kill him." Beatrice was very bold and firm in her response.

"Beatrice, I don't know what you are high on! But just know, I don't need your permission to do anything, okay? The whole country, and very soon the entire continent will be mine to rule. You shouldn't forget that you are only with that silly boy because you opted to watch him. It's not a real relationship."

"To you, it's not. Mom, you know how I feel about him." Beatrice said to her.

"Oh please. Spare me that crap!" Mrs. Nimako charged again.

"I am carrying his baby. A baby I am not going to raise alone. So no, you can't hurt or kill him." Beatrice revealed.

"What is making you think you are going to have that bastard's baby?" Mrs. Nimako said.

"Mom, it's a baby we are talking about. My baby. Did you get it? Beatrice was very upset.

"Beatrice, you have done worse things than killing an unborn baby. Abort that thing," Mrs. Nimako suggested politely.

"Not going to happen at any cost, Mom," Beatrice responded very firmly.

"I am working my ass off to make sure you guys are better before I leave this world. I want to see you and your sister have a perfect life. I am building an empire for you two to rule. I am a world for you. Open your eyes and see the bigger picture. You are queens and deserve to be treated as such. Don't let your emotions come in the way of business. What needs to be done must be done. That is how great men remain great. Can't you see you are your mother's child, and there is darkness in you. I am the tree, and you are my fruit, you can never fall far away from me" Mrs. Nimako said.

"I don't want it. If I have to rob people of their happiness because I want to rule, then I don't want it. There is no bigger picture Mom. You are becoming an autocrat and a tyrant. The power has corrupted you and that is not the life I imagined myself living. I am done... Oh, and also you know nothing about my darkness. But you will. And I am nothing like you Mom. I am tired of being another piece of your chessboard."

Beatrice was very angry in her response to her mother, Mrs. Nimako. She stormed out of the room. Mrs. Nimako got back on another call almost immediately.

"He is back in town. And I think he has it. Find him and find what he is possessing. When you do, end him for good." Mrs. Nimako instructed on the phone.

She hung up the phone and stared into the distance while she cracked her knuckles.

*****

Night fell at the motel. Kweku sat on the bed, watching the out-of-date television. Nkrumah was seated on the floor, playing with a tennis ball. They looked exhausted. The room was gradually getting messier. Rubbers and bottles of food are laid around.

Nkrumah's phone screen lit up at once. It was a message from Beatrice, her name had been saved with a lot of love and flower emojis. The new message that came in brought the screen display to thirty-eight missed calls and one hundred and thirty-two messages. All from the same person. He looked at his phone, tempted to respond to it but didn't. He watched the phone's light gently dim out as he calmed himself with the ball he had in his hand.

After a while of ignoring his phone, he finally attended to it. He opened the messages from Beatrice and scrolled to the very last one. It was a voice message. He played it.

"Nkrumah, I miss you. I know you don't want to talk to me but wherever you are I just want you to know that you are a wanted man. I am sorry for everything. I had no idea. If you decide to come home, you know where the keys will be. Call me, let's talk. Your baby says hi." The message read.

Nkrumah quickly put the phone down. He was in a confused state of mind; a part of him wanted to reconnect with Beatrice, but another part could not forgive her.

"You know you are supposed to get rid of that phone, right?" Kweku reminded Nkrumah.

"Yes, I will," Nkrumah replied.

Then they heard a very harsh knock. Kweku quickly grabbed his pistol. Nkrumah was also very alert.

"Who is there?" Kweku asked.

"It's your mom. Come on, open the door." Naruto replied.

Kweku and Nkrumah sighed a relief. Kweku opened the door to let her in.

"Jesus! Must you always be this scared? Anyway, Kweku, I brought your favorite." Naruto said.

She raised the rubber she was carrying in her hands.

"Fried yam and pork! I know, I am the best, right? Sir, I didn't know what you like, so I got you rice." Naruto said.

"Thank you. Just Nkrumah is fine. No sirs, no misters." Nkrumah said and smiled.

"Yes, please. Let's eat." Naruto replied.

They settled down. Everybody was at ease, enjoying their meals.

"So, in updates, I got the squad you asked for. Elite squad, rich blend of vigilante people, and a few ex-military men. Most of them were put off duty for misconduct but who cares? They have their own weapons, so that makes the work easier. The question right now is how do we pay for all of that." Naruto said.

Nkrumah smiled and reached for his bag. He pulled out a bar of gold. Kweku and Naruto's eyes were wide open, jaw dropped. That was gold! A big fat bar of gold.

"As I live and breathe," Naruto said in awe.

"Can you sell this on the dark net?" Nkrumah asked Naruto.

"Depends. How much is in it for me?" Naruto replied and asked.

"You can have it all. It's not the money that interests me. All I want is the head of the woman who took my parent's heads and wanted mine as well. I don't want to live the rest of my life in hiding, wondering when a sniper will be aiming at my head. I want to end this, for all of us." Nkrumah revealed.

"You have my support. I am tired of hiding." Kweku said.

"I have all the documents that will end them once and for all. But only Kwame Lots can make sense out of it." Nkrumah explained.

"Let's do it then. The final part of your plan. Operation Rescue Kwame Lots." Naruto said.

"It's not only Kwame there. A lot more people. If we get them out and they tell their stories, it's over for the VPC and their evil queen mother." Nkrumah said.

That same night in Nkrumah's house. Beatrice was seated on the floor. The television lights flicked onto her high face. She was smoking a roll of weed. One roll which had already been burnt out lay on the glass center table. Two other untouched rolls on there. Beatrice was high. Every single cell in her body was high.

She went at it for a while and then the doorbell rang.

"Go home. There is no one here." Said, Beatrice.

Eric let himself in and his mood suddenly dipped after he saw Beatrice in the state she was. He had never seen her like that. If not for then, he could hardly imagine something of that sort happening.

"Madam Madonna. What has come over you?" Eric asked.

"It's a party. Come on, sit." Beatrice told Eric.

"I got your text. What was your emergency?" Eric asked.

Beatrice passed him a roll of the weed. She smiled and laughed and giggled, and Eric didn't even know how to react to all of that.

"No thank you. I am fine." Eric said and rejected the roll of weed.

"Come on. Don't be boring. I insist, please." Beatrice said.

Eric put it into a little thought. Rolled his eyes and then took the roll.

"There we go," Beatrice said and smiled.

Eric took a long sip. He was the more experienced of the two and the comfort at which he handled and went about the business made it evident. It hit him at the right spot.

"Damn. This is good." Eric praised.

"I know, right," Beatrice took pride in her words.

"So, tell me. What is it that couldn't wait?" Eric asked.

"Yeah. About that," Beatrice replied as she pointed to the roll of weed.

"When did you get this? You need to put me on your plug." Eric said while he smoked.

"Focus bro," Beatrice told Eric.

"My paddy. Hit me." Eric said.

"I want to stand for president if you help me, "Beatrice suggested.

"For the VPC?" Eric asked.

"No dummy. Against the VPC," Beatrice replied.

"Okay. I think you've had a little too much. Come on, let me get you to your bed."

"No. I know what I am saying. My mother is a self-centered selfish woman who wants everything to herself."

"Come on. We are not having this conversation. You don't know what you are saying," Eric said.

"Ain't you tired of being slave to this party? We can end all of these. Me and you." Beatrice lauded.

"Bea. Your mother is the most powerful person in this country. Every official, every agency, every institution is in her pocket. The ECOWAS and even the African Union worship her. That is the kind of figure we are dealing with here. I understand your frustration, this whole thing frustrates me too. But this is not your fight, neither is it mine. We can just consider ourselves lucky we are on the winning team." Eric explained.

"I don't want to win like that. That is not a winning team. My mother will destroy everything and anything to get what she wants. She will tear this country apart. Can't you see?"

"No. The only thing I can see right now is you are high as fuck, saying things you won't even remember in the morning." Eric replied.

"I am not high."

"Tell that to your eyes." Eric teased her.

He went to pick the rest of the rolls from the table.

"These are coming with me. And I am trusting you to be responsible enough to stay out of trouble. Get some rest, Beatrice," Eric advised.

He walked out of the place. Beatrice slid down the couch with her back till she got her back lying flat on the floor.

"They are scared. Everybody is scared. But I am not," She said to herself.

Chapter 11

It was night in the motel. Naruto was busy. She typed at a very high speed and made a lot of noise as she tapped the keys of her laptop. Nkrumah strolled the room in discomfort. He looked like a man who couldn't wait any longer.

Kweku was rather calm in his zone, watching a football match on the television.

"How many minutes out?" Nkrumah asked Naruto.

"Can't tell precisely. Roughly 7, 10, I don't know. Calm down. They are professionals. They will find him." Naruto replied.

Nkrumah couldn't calm down. He continued pacing the room. Passed in front of Kweku over and over. He was restless. Kweku who had had enough but could not complain, changed the channel. A Mexican opera. He changed again, the music video again. Then one more and the news was on.

"If you've still not heard, earlier today something out of this world happened. Miss Beatrice Nimako, second daughter of the founder of the VPC, today submitted her bid to run for president to the electoral commission with just four and a half months to elections. This put the whole country in a state of shock and surprise as her submission was to run as an independent candidate against her mother's party. Out of nowhere, what looked to be a one-horse race has changed." The newscaster read on the television.

"What!" Kweku was puzzled.

"Turn that off," Nkrumah said.

Nkrumah walked to the television and did it himself.

"Guys. We are in the middle of a very big night. We can't be distracted. Everything is at stake here, for all we know, this is another move to favor themselves. All of these are a game to these people. But we are done playing, Naruto please, update." Nkrumah said.

"They are close. Real close." Naruto replied.

"Good. Let's bring Kwame home." Nkrumah said.

Same moment two pickup cars drove through the woods. The car in the front had two people, one drove and another one in the front seat. Two other men sat in the trunk part of the pickup. They held rifles in their hands. The whole team was dressed as a militia unit. Same with the second car.

Yussif was the leader of the militia group. He had a scar on his face from a long time ago. He was the man seated in the front seat of the first car. He looked at a tablet which displays a map. They followed a green dot on the map. A dot that was close to the position of the car. As the position of their car looked to have laid over the green dot, he ordered the car to a halt and then came down. The rest of the team joined him on the ground. Eight of them, all armed and strapped.

"We are here. I see nothing that is of interest to you over." Yussif talked into a walkie-talkie.

"You can't see any building at all. Even if it's an old abandoned one. Over." Naruto replied into walkie-talkie.

"Nothing yet. But I will search the perimeter. I will keep you updated. Over and out." Yussif said and got off the walkie.

"GPS says whoever we are looking for is close enough. Spread out, don't go more than three hundred meters away. If you see anything report to me." Yussif commanded.

"Yes Sir." They all responded in no particular order as they dispersed to search. All of them with touches in their hands. Yussif remained put. By his side was the driver of the first car.

"Boss. Any idea what we are looking for? Is it worth all the trouble?" The driver was curious.

"We don't ask the questions, my boy. We answer them. And right now, the question here is where is the bloody whoever we have been tasked to get and we will answer that."

"Yes Sir." The driver said.

Back to the motel room. A very tense atmosphere. Nkrumah tapped his feet in frustration. Finger in his mouth. Fidgeting all over. Kweku had his prayer rosary in his hands at that point. Dragged on slowly as he looked to have loosed faith in the mission.

Naruto looked at both men and felt the uneasiness they felt.

"We will get them guys. We will get them." Naruto assured them.

Back to the woods, where Yussif and his men were. Yussif was still put on the lookout. One of his men rushed to him.

"Sir we found something."

"We found something. Going to inspect." Yussif reported to Naruto over the walkie-talkie.

A few seconds later, the militia man led Yussif and the other two men to a tree where a dead body hanged. It was Kwame Lots. It looked like he had been like that for quite a while. Yussif called it in.

"Positive. We found something." Yussif reported to Naruto over the walkie-talkie.

"A building. Please tell me it's a building." Nkrumah said over the walkie-talkie. He felt very tense.

"A person," Yussif replied.

"Kwame Lots! Ask him if his name is Kwame Lots" Nkrumah said.

"He is dead," Yussif replied.

Kweku, Nkrumah, and Naruto all reacted to the unfortunate news back at the motel room. Nkrumah felt it the most. He slowly paced backward, goosebumps all over his body. A bead of tears rolled down Kweku's face almost immediately. Nkrumah went to the wall and sat with his back against it and then screamed out in pain.

"Nooo! We failed him. I failed him," Nkrumah cried out.

"Baddest, should we bring the body?" Yussif asked Naruto over the walkie-talkie.

The place was quiet. Everybody was in their emotional distress.

"Baddest. Should we bring the body, over?" Yussif asked again.

"Let them bring it. I know his son," Kweku said in tears.

"Bring it home Yussif," Naruto replied over the walkie-talkie.

"Copy that. The Zebra team signing out. Over and out." Yussif said.

"This can't be it. There should be something else we can do," Naruto closed the laptop and thought to herself.

"This is it. The VPC wins again." Nkrumah said.

He seemed to have lost hope.

"So what happens to your evidence? We still have that, don't we?" Naruto asked.

"Everything we have is useless without Kwame Lots. He is the only one who can make sense out of all these madness. I know nothing." Nkrumah said furiously.

The place went quiet. Everyone grieved silently.

"Kwame Lots was the best thing that happened to me. I met him as an intern. I owe my career to him." Kweku cried.

"May his soul rest in peace! What do we do now?" Naruto asked.

"Nothing. It's the VPC. There is nothing we can do." Nkrumah replied.

"So what happens to you two?" Naruto further asked.

"I don't know. Maybe I give them what they want in exchange for my life." Nkrumah replied in a very confused way.

"And me?" Kweku asked.

"I can give you all the money you will need. To go far away and start a new life." Nkrumah stated.

"I can work on a new identity for you. But I don't think any of you should run, or surrender. Stand on your feet and fight." Naruto said.

"You don't get it. Its the VPC and Mrs. Nimako. Anything you say is rubbish. Do you know how many people have tried?" Nkrumah said.

"Nkrumah is right. A few papers won't prove anything. Especially when we don't know what it is even about," Kweku added.

Nkrumah punched the ground severally. Tried to channel out all the hurt he felt but there was just too much of it.

Nkrumah finally came home after his coup attempt didn't surface. He stood in front of the house, broke out heavily, and nursed his broken heart.

Then he went for the keys from under one of the flowerpots seated in front of the house. He entered the room and at once caught an awkward vibe.

"Hello." He called out.

He looked around suspiciously. The button of weed rolls still lay on the table. As he still inspected what seemed unusual, he wandered into the kitchen, where a card lay on the dining table. It read, *"CALL THIS NUMBER IF YOU WANT YOUR BABY."* He was alarmed at once. He picked up the card and rushed to the landline phone and called the number on there.

"I was wondering when you will call." It was Abigail's voice on the phone at the other end.

"Abigail?" Nkrumah was puzzled.

"Hi, baby," Abigail replied.

"What is this? What is all of these about?" Nkrumah asked.

He heard Beatrice's voice in the background.

"Don't give them shit," Beatrice said in the background.

"I guess that saves me a long frightening speech. You might not care about her, but she carries your baby. You know what we want. Bring it and in exchange, we give you the so-called love of your life. Think about it." Abigail proposed in a threatening voice.

"Wait! I want to meet you. Let's do the exchange in person. I can't trust anyone with this." Nkrumah begged her.

"That's fine with me. Call me when you're ready. I will give you a location. You don't need to disclose it or to tell anyone. Come alone. I hope I'm clear enough." Abigail said and cut the call abruptly.

Nkrumah's broken heart deepened. He thought to himself. What must he do? And then in the middle of all of that, a random idea hit him. It brought some life into him. He at once became sharper. He pulled a pocket notebook and then made a call.

The call rang, no response. It went straight to voicemail.

"Naruto. Get to Kweku and tell him I need him to call in a few hours. I need to see you as soon as possible."

Chapter 12

Beatrice was tied into a chair in what looked to be an abandoned warehouse. Abigail sat there and played with her phone.

"Why are you doing this?" Beatrice asked Abigail.

"Sorry baby. I didn't hear that," Abigail responded.

She stood up and headed straight to Beatrice.

"Say that again," Abigail said.

Beatrice was teary. Her sister? Never in a thousand years would she have imagined.

"What is this? Who is making you do this? Mummy?" Beatrice cried out.

"No. Make no mistakes. I am doing this for me. To make my point." Abigail said.

"And that is what exactly?" Beatrice asked.

"That I am not weak. I am not some nerd who is supposed to be doing the numbers. I am the big sister. It's my birthright to be in the spotlight." Abigail said.

Beatrice got puzzled.

"What! That is what this is? Take it. Take all of it. I didn't want any of this and I still don't. This is not who you are, Abigail. Does Mom even know about this?" Beatrice asked.

"You are running against her for God's sake, do you think she will care? I am tired of you always winning everything. You are always the diva, and me, just another girl in the background holding your gown."

"God, Abigail! Are you listening to yourself?" Beatrice was surprised.

"You are tied up now and I will be the queen. Refreshing!" Abigail teased.

"A Queen? That is the lecture Mom gave you? It will destroy you. Our mother is a selfish gold digger," Beatrice said.

"No. It is you who has lost sight. Look at the bigger picture," Abigail responded with confident.

"There is no bigger picture, big sister. There is just Mrs. Nimako's picture."

Abigail smiled sarcastically.

"Like I said. You have lost sight." Abigail angrily said and punched Beatrice in the face.

Night fell at the warehouse. Beatrice stood with a gun aimed at her head. Abigail was the one with the gun. Nkrumah was then escorted on by two men. There was a sack over his head, and he couldn't see through. He held in his hands the rusty box that the documents came with. The two men took off his head sack. As soon as he saw Beatrice, he tried to run toward her.

"Hey, hey, hey. Not a step. Stand put." Abigail warned.

Nkrumah stepped back.

"I asked to see your mother. Where is she?" Nkrumah asked.

"Hand that over," Abigail commanded Nkrumah.

"Not until I speak with Mrs. Nimako," Nkrumah replied.

"I am sorry." Beatrice apologized.

"Hey, don't be," Nkrumah said.

"Of course, she is. She is sorry for spying on you for five-plus years. Watching you, forcing you to believe she loves you." Abigail revealed.

"She did love me. She still does." Nkrumah defended Beatrice.

Mrs. Nimako walked on from behind Abigail. "Well, well, well... Nice scene as the love birds standing before each other..." Mrs. Nimako said.

"Look at you. You had so much promise. Look at what following your feelings have led you to." Mrs. Nimako addressed Beatrice.

"To you my baby. You have done me proud." She praised Abigail.

"Leave us." She commanded the guards.

The two guards left the scene.

"Shall we? Hand them over." Mrs. Nimako said.

"Did you kill my father?" Nkrumah asked.

"There could be a sniper anywhere aimed at your head." Mrs. Nimako said.

"I am not afraid of death." Nkrumah boldly responded.

"Ha!... I always wondered what my daughter saw in you to stick around that long. Five years. She was to investigate you for a year. But I see it now." Mrs. Nimako confirmed.

"Did you kill my father?" Nkrumah asked again.

"Of course, I did. I stabbed the son of a bitch countless times because he crossed me. Nobody crosses me. I have done worse things and God knows I will do worse things. I am a god, and nobody dares stand in my way." Mrs. Nimako bragged.

"Abigail, is that the woman you want to be?" Beatrice asked Abigail.

"Shut up Beatrice... Now I won't ask again. Hand the damn thing over!" Mrs. Nimako warned.

"Why do you need it?" Nkrumah asked.

Mrs. Nimako who slowly ran out of patience pulled out a kitchen knife, pushed Abigail out of the way, and then placed it on Beatrice's neck.

Abigail was shocked. What was happening? Beatrice began to breathe heavily. She knew her mother couldn't do it.

"Do it. I dare you. She is your daughter, not mine." Nkrumah dared Mrs. Nimako.

"Nkrumah, no! She has your baby." Abigail said.

"I have the instrument to make another," Nkrumah responded.

"Mom, please. It hasn't gotten to this." Abigail pleaded.

"You are willing to kill your daughter over some stupid papers?" Nkrumah asked.

"You have five seconds to push that over... Five! Four!" Mrs. Nimako counted down.

Nkrumah didn't look like he wanted to surrender.

"Three…" Mrs. Nimako continued the count.

"What are you doing? Give it her." Abigail yelled at Nkrumah.

Abigail had her pistol aimed at Nkrumah.

"Two…" Mrs. Nimako went on the count.

"Mom please." Abigail pleaded.

"I love you, Nkrumah." Beatrice cried out in tears.

"One." Mrs. Nimako ended the count!

"Wait!" Nkrumah screamed.

Everybody sighed a relief. Nkrumah placed the box down on the floor.

"You sent men to kill me because of this. You killed my father because of this. Why should I let you kill because of this? Your actions make me think there is something that can destroy you in there." Nkrumah said.

Nkrumah kicked the box. It slid across the ground and Mrs. Nimako stopped it by putting her hand on it.

"I am guessing your plan was to kill me as soon as I handed it to you. But I came up with a better plan." Nkrumah said.

Abigail who instinctively felt all of those were traps began to get even more scared.

"What is happening? What are you talking about?" Abigail asked.

"At the moment this conversation is playing on live radio. Outside this gate, a news team is standing by to get you on video." Nkrumah revealed.

"That's a bluff. I have men all over the perimeter." Mrs. Nimako said and laughed bossily.

"You brought a few trusted men. I brought a sixteen-man army. Do you still want to talk about men?" Nkrumah asked.

"Come in." He called the men.

Bang! The door to the place was forcefully opened. The sixteen-man army came and surrounded them. Kweku walked in with a camera crew.

"Remember me?" Kweku asked Mrs. Nimako. But she never replied

"We are issuing a citizen's arrest on you, Mrs. Akosua Nimako. Your end has come."

The men arrested all three women, Mrs. Akosua Nimako and her two daughters.

The country celebrated. They finally had the freedom they had longed for. All the officials of the VPC were arrested and prosecuted. But Beatrice was given bail because of her pregnancy. The VPC party was dissolved. The underworld was discovered, and the prisoners were freed. Several political parties emerged and submitted their nominations for the presidential race. The Freedom Party won, and the president offered Beatrice a presidential pardon.

Some months later, Beatrice gave birth to a boy. Nkrumah and Beatrice got married and lived happily. Kweku Asante was honored the communication minister in the new government.

Acknowledgement

My heartfelt thanks go to my good friend, my mentor, and my uncle, Shrikrishna Singh, PhD. He is the reason I am who I am today. His genuine inspiration, encouragement, and mentorship brought my talent to life. Without him, this book would never have happened. I want to thank my family, the Koku Gyata family. I would also express my gratitude to my friends, Gloria and Jennifer, for their genuine support. It would be tantamount to absolute gross ingratitude if this book is accomplished without registering my thankfulness to Auctus Publishers and its owner, Shrikrishna Singh, PhD, for his **sincere** encouragement and genuine support of my writing passion.